OFF KECK ROAD

ALSO BY MONA SIMPSON

~

A Regular Guy

The Lost Father

Anywhere But Here

OFF KECK ROAD

~

Mona Simpson

Alfred A. Knopf / New York

2 0 0 0

THIS IS A BORZOI BOOK

PUBLISHED BY ALFRED A. KNOPF

www.aaknopf.com

Knopf, Borzoi Books, and the colophon
are registered trademarks of Random House, Inc.

Library of Congress Cataloging-in-Publication Data
Simpson, Mona.
Off Keck Road / Mona Simpson. — 1st ed.
p.   cm.
ISBN 0-375-41010-4 (alk. paper)
1. Women—Wisconsin—Green Bay—Fiction.   2. Mothers and daughters—
Fiction.   3. Female friendship—Fiction.   4. Green Bay (Wis.)—Fiction.   I. Title.
PS3569.I5117 O35 2000
813'.54—dc21   00-040569

Manufactured in the United States of America
First Edition

for Richard Appel and Allan Gurganus

The author would like to thank Alfred Appel Jr., Cristina Garcia, Robert Cohen, Amanda Urban, Cecily Hillsdale, Elma Dayrit, Robert Grover, her colleagues at Bard College, the Lila Wallace–Reader's Digest Foundation, and especially Gary Fisketjon, but for whom this small volume would not exist.

OFF KECK ROAD

I

*B*ea Maxwell remembered the first time she'd driven out to see the new part of town. It was 1956 and she was home from college for the winter break. After Christmas, though, she *had* to get away from the house. Her sister and her sister's entourage had taken over the place. Her sister always traveled with an entourage. And it was still nine days before Bea could return to the sorority in Madison.

Bea had friends from high school, too, quiet girls who were back from other colleges, even a few who had stayed in town, working in the kindergartens or at the hospital or for Kendalls, the big department store, but these were not the people she wanted to see. She needed someone from Madison, to touch that part of her life. So she'd called June Umberhum.

June sounded glad to hear from her. She was going stir-crazy, too, she said.

Just then, someone else came on the line. A farmer's wife June said she'd never even seen, who lived somewhere farther out.

"Well, how much longer are you going to be?" that woman asked.

"Just a jiff," June said.

"Already been on a quarter hour."

After she hung up—rather loudly, Bea thought—they hurried to make their plans.

June wanted downtown. They agreed on Kaap's, for ice cream.

But Wednesday morning, June telephoned. Her brother and his awful girlfriend, Nance, had driven the only car up north. Both her sisters were working. No one could run her in. Bus service from Green Bay didn't reach that far out yet.

Where she lived was not part of the city proper. It was still Prebble, but there was already a motion to incorporate the village into the city charter.

"Probly never happen," June said. "Or when we're forty."

But three days before, Bea had got her own car, a 1956 Oldsmobile Holiday, red, her Christmas present. She could go and fetch June.

On the party line, though, June sounded stingy giving directions.

"I can walk to the highway and meet you somewhere. Or should we just make it another day?"

When Bea insisted she wanted to take the car for a spin anyway, June sighed. "Oh, okay."

It was a bright cold day with a weak blue sky. It wasn't snowing anymore but it had and the white was everywhere, glaring off in planes, making flat surfaces of things ordinarily rounded. Bea wore driving gloves with holes cut out for the knuckles—her other present, from Elaine, although she was sure her mother had picked them and seen that they were gift wrapped—and her mood lifted as she drove past the stately houses, away from the quaint, pretty downtown. The specialty shops (Vander Zanden's Fine Jewelry, Jandrain's Formal and Bridal) had the ravaged feel of the boxes still under the Christmas tree in her own house. She knew their contents.

She heard the regularly spaced girders of the bridge click under her new tires. Once you came down off the ramp on Mason, you passed a number of old buildings that happened to grow up near one another; they were clearly not built to look any way together or to make up a "downtown." There was a cheese factory with a sour smell and a canning plant, with small windows and two large chimneys, operating today, judging from the squiggles of white smoke on the blank sky. They'd reopened already or perhaps the factories didn't close for Christmas, as the small shops did.

Then there was a low bank of brick storefronts; Bea spotted a selection of electric organs, sparkly green and gray, inside one—the Music Mecca, where people also went to take lessons.

She drove farther east on Highway 141, which was what Main Street turned into.

"That road was never any good," Bea's mother would say, and as long as Bea could remember, it had not been.

In 1956, the highway had a junk store, a truly immense dilapidated place that reminded Bea of a banked ship. She could vaguely make out a man inside, carrying a stick, moving amid the dim jumble.

She passed a motel, two-storied, with a slim twirled railing along the top floor. The son of the people who lived there, behind the lobby, had gone to high school with June. He was also the Maxwell's paperboy.

The Starlight Supper Club had a ball revolving on top of a tower, set over the octagonal dining room. There was a drive-in movie theater, which advertised FRIDAY NIGHT FISH FRY on a home-painted sign. And of course Kroll's, a rectangular building of yellow and maroon tiles, where teenagers for two generations had gone for malteds and chili dogs. Bea's mother had been taken there on dates, in her youth. "When I was dating" was as clear an era in Bea's mother's life as when she was in grade school or when her own children were still in diapers.

By the time Bea came to the part of the highway that ended June's road, she felt she'd already left town. There was a deep snow over everything, and when she turned onto Keck Road, she had to slow down. It was cleared out by hand. She could see the rows a shovel blade had made, two feet wide.

The city snowplows wouldn't come this far, either. On one corner, there was a white farmhouse, and on the other, a small tavern, pink and gray, that looked like an ordinary house during the daytime. Children's boots drooped on the porch. A little farther up, the plowed middle of the road narrowed, and on top of the icy snow were sprigs of hay.

The road was paved only as far as there were houses, eight in all. From where she was, Bea could see the road ending, and beyond that, fields led down to the railroad tracks.

The houses looked small and hastily built, but the land out here was magnificent. Her mother would have loved to see the trees. A Norway spruce was half again as tall as the tree in front of City Hall, the one lit with candles at the annual Monk's Charity Carol on Christmas Eve.

Sun glittered on crusted snow, a forbidding brightness. Even in the intricate construction of ice and crystals, there was the promise of a green melting, change.

. . .

And everywhere here, there were children, children running, children rolling snowballs, children on lumber they used as toboggans, children jumping off a shed into banks of snow so deep they turned invisible to Bea when they landed.

They seemed scantily dressed and altogether unattended, some downright wild, such as the one swinging from a bare hickory branch, which looked like it could break any minute, some fifteen feet above the snow. That child, like many others, was not wearing mittens.

The claustrophobia Bea had felt since the indoors day of Christmas swept out of her. She rolled down the new car's window (inside the chrome handle, a circle of red leather). This vigor outdoors looked to her like a painting she had seen projected up on the auditorium screen at college, a Brueghel sparked to life.

A thin-ankled, pregnant woman stepped out of one of the small houses, carrying a baby. She walked down the driveway and put a letter in the mailbox, just a few feet away from Bea's car. The baby, with a brown mark on its eyelid, couldn't have been more than a few months old. Could she have been that pregnant again already?

Bea felt like getting out and tromping in the snow. She thought of her cross-country skis leaning in the garage at home.

June, the sorority sweetheart (literally, she was that; Bea had voted for her in Green Bay solidarity), June—who wore a sparkling blue-and-gold sari to the house invitational—lived here! Perhaps she'd been one of these antic children.

Bea would not be invited into June's house, not this time. On the other side of the road, there was a semicircular driveway before a pretty two-story white house. There, under the most spectacular tree Bea had ever seen, June stood like a tiny queen, stamping her feet in fur-trimmed boots.

Her whole body leapt into motion as she opened the door and flew into Bea's new red car.

"Let's go," June said.

From there, they talked a mile a minute—nothing about their Christmases, nothing about their homes, only about people they knew in Madison.

But Bea wondered, in a scant way, as she glanced in her rearview mirror, about to turn onto that bad highway, what would become of these ruddy, unminded children.

II

*I*n the obituary for Jonas Salk, run by the Green Bay *Press Gazette*, the wire service reporter said that by 1963, we had wiped out polio in the United States.

Except Shelley. She must have been one of the last people to contract the disease. Now, they said in that same article, polio is coming back again.

Shelley knows the exact day she got it. It was a May Saturday in 1961, the year the oral vaccine was introduced. She was five years old.

On Saturday mornings, Shelley's father would corral the kids, give the wife a chance to rest her feet.

Not that the wife did. She usually went on a long walk with another lady so they could yak, yak, yak. When Shelley's father said this, he'd shake his head to mean he didn't understand it. A favorite joke of his was, "Too bad the two of youse can't get married."

The vaccinations were given in a high school gymnasium, free, over on their side of town.

The gym doubled as the auditorium. At one end of the big room, there was a stage where the nurses stood, injecting for tetanus and passing out small paper cups with the polio vaccine. The front half of the line received the vaccine in sugar cubes, pink or blue, one inside each Dixie cup. After those ran out, the nurses poured a certain measured amount of a sweet liquid. It was all very matter-of-fact. The disposable needles came wrapped in paper, like tampons, packed in square boxes. Beside each nurse was her own wastebasket.

Kids waited in a long line on the part of the floor painted for basketball. Against the wall was a half-built float, a covered wagon, the cloth made of square school-issue toilet paper stuffed into the hexagonal openings of chicken wire. It would take hundreds of hours to fill the wire honeycomb with white paper blossoms.

"*Girl work,*" Shelley's middle brother said with a down-turning mouth.

High school girls did it, probably all the while thinking of themselves sitting on top, dressed up as pioneer women or some such thing, waving to a big crowd. Nell Umberhum would most likely be the one to ride on it. And she wouldn't have helped build it, either. She had a paying job already, waitressing at Kroll's.

Shelley's older sister, Kim, drifted over to touch.

They were four children then. Dean hadn't been born yet. He came five years later, a last surprise, and, like a present, he was the one who always was so handsome. Bea Maxwell had been wrong that afternoon in 1956. Shelley's mother's belly still looked full from having been pregnant with Shelley.

She'd been wrong about another thing, too. It was not the first time she'd seen Keck Road. Once, in elementary school, she and her best friend had collected food for the poor. They'd been driven out to hand the grocery bags over to a family in an apricot-colored house with all kinds of junk in the front yard. That time, the street had looked different, terrifying.

It seemed to Shelley and her sister and brothers that they could move about and still keep their place in line. Their mother would've let them. She tried to give them every advantage of being a four-kid family. She believed that small families were sad—in all cases, the result of selfishness or medical tragedy. And she trusted the world to help raise her children. If she'd been there, she would have already been talking to another mother. Her main public service in the world was that—being a mother—and she felt she was a good one.

But her husband stood with his arms folded tight. He didn't want anyone to suppose his kids were cutting in line.

Shelley's brothers signaled to other guys who ran track and to Petey from across the road, standing on his head twenty yards in front of them, next to his mom.

The line moved, but it was so long. Shelley kept looking at her feet, happy because she had new sneakers. She was already as tall as Kim, but two years younger. She got these shoes because she'd grown out of last summer's already. Her goal was to get so that Kim would have to wear her hand-me-downs, even though Shelley was the youngest, a goal she would soon achieve.

Kim tried to step on Shelley's tennies to make marks. Their mother would have noticed, even through her conversation with the other mother, would've turned to say "*Stopit*," but their dad just lifted a hand, as if they were each equally to blame.

Shelley's feet kept dancing to miss her sister's. So far, she was doing it. Her sneakers were clean.

When they were getting close to the front, three S's away, June Umberhum rushed in with her daughter, Peggy. They all knew Peggy because June often left her with the grandma, and sometimes the grandma paid Kim and Shelley a quarter to keep an eye on her while she did her housework. They watched for June's white Volkswagen coming down Keck Road.

Peggy tiptoed ahead of her mother, but not too far, like dice or jacks thrown from a hand.

She was in white: white shorts, a white top, white anklets, white tennies, and a white bow in her hair. She was only two years old and everything she had on was new.

Looking at her made Shelley not care much anymore about marks on her shoes. They would come anyway, sooner or later. Soon.

When June first returned to Green Bay, their mother had given her their hand-me-downs for Peggy. June had stood by the open door of her white VW (the seats covered in red plaid!) and said, "Oh, thanks. These'll come in handy." But they never once saw Peggy wearing anything of theirs.

Now their mother gave their old clothes to the church.

But June still fascinated them. Especially Kim—who tried to make her own hair curl up at the ends the way June's did. (June probably copied it from an actress on TV.) "I bet she has a standing appointment at the beauty shop," Kim said.

That day in the high school gym, June was wearing sunglasses and high heels and pants. Shelley hadn't ever seen high heels before with pants. And sunglasses! She stood out in the underwater gymnasium light.

She went right up in a movie-star way to their dad and said, "Hi, Tommy," and just started standing with them, her arms crossed like his.

The children looked—no one else called their father Tommy.

She probably thought she could do this, always having been pretty and being one of the ones who got to go off to college. She didn't seem to know—the way the other women here did—that being pretty had an end date, like milk. A year past twenty-three and already having had a kid swim through her body, she was past fresh. But she took the privileges just the same. And Thomas didn't know how to stop her.

His crossed arms tightened and his children understood that she was cutting in line and he was thinking, What about the people behind? What were *they* going to say? His children's scurrying subsided. Their mother could have solved all this with just a lift of her eyebrow to the woman in front of her.

That signal would have meant many things and would have been repeated, like Telephone, all the way down the line: *Who does she think she is? At her age. With a kid yet. And everyone knowing he ran off. But good for her, I guess, too. Maybe the rules aren't the rules always. Heck, maybe even for us.*

Thomas's mouth sank. June was asking what he thought of the vaccine, wasn't it something what Salk had done, all kinds of round shapes and bright colors in her voice, and he wouldn't look down at her face. He'd drop a word when he had to, just a pellet, one at a time.

Then June saw her sister-in-law with Petey. "Oh, *there* they are!" she shouted, and opened her hand twice to her daughter, then pulled her by the arm up to the front of the line.

Their dad's mouth loosened as he watched her go.

If they had stayed, the order would have been different. Someone else would have received Shelley's cup.

They all left together, June, Nance, and the two cousins, Petey doubling over to walk out on his hands.

Then, a little while later, they stepped up to the plate in order. Butch first, flinching, then Timmy, brave, just shoving up his shirtsleeve. Kim next, looking away from the quick needle. Then Shelley. They had to stand there and drink the whole cupful. The nurse waited until the paper dropped into the wastebasket. The liquid tasted like cherry syrup.

Shelley looked up at the nurse's clean face. She wasn't like her sister, afraid for a pin-second hurt. She gazed at her with trust, glad to be next. The nurse unpeeled the circus Band-Aid and gave a smile she'd saved. "Littlest one and bravest of all," she said after Shelley drank the cup down. "Don't forget your sucker."

On the way out, they each got a sucker. Hers was orange.

As soon as she started unfurling the wrapper, Kim jumped on the front of her left foot. "Ha!"

Shelley never considered what would have happened if Peggy and June had waited their turn at the end of the line. When she did compare luck, it was with her sister. (Her family was the world then.)

And she was never able to keep the facts straight. She thought it was the shot that gave her the disease and the cup of potion that compensated, making it just a little. She also believed, although her mother and dad told her differently, that the polio had caused the brown spot above her eye.

People thought you got it from not being clean. One of the ladies from the church came out and told Shelley's mother it was because she didn't wash her vegetables. And that wasn't true. She always washed.

In those days, they thought it wasn't quite as good to eat garden food you grew at home. Everybody knew at the canning factory they sanitized with heat.

Other people thought the polio came from swimming in the public pools. But out where they lived, they didn't swim in pools. There was a public pool in a park but you had to pay to get in, and then it was another quarter to get the locker key. Plus it was driving distance away. Shelley and her brothers swam in creeks and quarries, wherever they found clear water.

On the other side of the river, in a cluttered office, Dr. Herbert Maxwell gave the vaccinations one at a time, to children whose mothers brought them in by appointment. In 1961, he still gave shots for polio. He hadn't switched over to the live vaccine. (Two years later, he would add it, keeping Salk's as a booster shot.) None of the children on the register from his practice contracted the disease during the years he performed inoculations. In his file marked "Polio" was an article he'd clipped and underlined. *"Before releasing the vaccine, Jonas Salk tested it in 1953 on himself and his own family, his wife and his three sons."*

III

hat they said about Shelley on Keck Road was, *She's always by the gramma. She just likes the gramma.*

Even Shelley didn't know how it started. Her dad told her she used to walk over to her grandmother's house when she was only three or four. So it started before her leg was heavy or her smile dragged to the left.

When Shelley was old enough to go to school, she worried about what her gramma had to do all day while Shelley, always the tallest, was sitting at her desk at the back, so bored that time became granular, round balls to touch and count. She thought her gramma and the grandmother across the road should do something together, whatever old ladies did.

Gram Umberhum lived next to her married son, George. She wore rubber boots halfway up to her knees, and overalls. Shelley's gramma put on stockings even under her robe, so her legs were the color of dark toast. She once told Shelley, "Always wear stockings. Under anything. Even pants." There had been anxiety in the instruction—a comb lightly pressed into the skin of her arm.

But even different, both ladies were grandmas, old and alone.

Shelley thought her gramma might like to have a friend. They could go someplace together to eat, or join a card club where at the end they served a fancy dessert.

Shelley loved her grandmother the way you love only one person, the person who would put your life over anything else. When her grandmother died, Shelley understood she would never be that way again, set apart.

When Shelley suggested her gramma call the other grandmother on the telephone to make a plan, she answered, "She's got her life and I've got mine."

That made sense to Shelley, as everything her gramma said did, only because she said it. Later, when Shelley thought of it, she told herself, *Neither of them two had much of any life*. But they did, she supposed. Just a kind of life that was hard to see.

The two old ladies sometimes met when they walked out to their mailboxes. On those occasions, they stood on the road and talked.

Once, when Shelley and Kim were over there baby-sitting, Peggy asked why their uncle Bob didn't live with their gramma.

Uncle Bob lived in the apartment over their gramma's garage. In there was a room with a kitchen, and his own pots and pans hung on nails in the wall. Sometimes her gramma would cook extra for him and give it to Shelley to carry up in a pot.

Why didn't they live together? It was hard to say why, but they wouldn't. They just never would.

"It's her brother, not her husband," Gram Umberhum explained, turning from her stove. "There the husband's dead, just like me."

The children were silent, absorbing the knowledge. Only husbands and wives lived together. Not brothers and sisters, when they were old. This still left questions. Why did Shelley's gramma live in a nice house, with carpeting and her own TV in the living room and all the things houses had, and him in a room more like a shack, up in the garage?

For that, nobody gave them any answer, and they knew enough not to ask.

Shelley was her gramma's favorite. After school, she went over and her gramma would fix her a liverwurst sandwich, slice it in four and cut the crusts off.

"You don't have to do that," Shelley always said. "I eat crust."

Her gramma would open the kitchen window and throw the crusts out onto the snow, for the birds.

After her snack Shelley would go out and work in the yard. She and her dad took care of the outside for her gramma. Shelley was the one who learned. Her oldest brother, Butch, tried, but their dad always scolded and he'd end up running inside. Pretty soon, they started calling him Boo Boo because he was always blubbering. Her second brother, Timmy, could do anything, but from when he was seven or eight, he was working for the nurseries, for pay. In summer, Shelley mowed; in fall, she raked; in winter, she shoveled. Even with the polio, she was strong. She once hacked a boulder out of her gramma's garden and hauled it all the way out front, next to the mailbox, before anyone noticed.

Her gramma would make dinner. She never let Shelley help her cook or even do the dishes. Shelley waited in the living room for everything to be on the table, the way a man would after coming back from work.

She walked home from her gramma's when it was falling dark. Between the two houses, there was old land. To Shelley, that undivided land meant the seasons. In autumn, it looked like Halloween, the big branches black, orange in the sunset sky. Later in the year, it would become a dark, clear blue.

During a storm, her grandmother stood at her door, watching her, her little porch lamp on, making the snow where the light fell look fake, like Styrofoam.

They didn't have sidewalks. When it was clear, small stars were so numerous and bright, Shelley could hardly believe she wouldn't have something in her hand just from seeing them.

Winter was the longest season where they lived. At dusk, there were depths in the banks of snow, curves upon curves, a frozen sea, blue and more blue receding out the long plains, with no edges. The snow softened roofs and silos, blunting trees, shearing particulars as far as you could see.

If you were outside, you were apt to be alone. There was the poignance of ending and faint yellow lights in the distance.

Somewhere else, women were cooking in kitchens. Miles from here, men sat stiff-armed, driving their cars.

You could see: The world would freeze again before it melted.

Her mother always sighed when she saw Shelley come in, thinking how she could best use another pair of hands. There was always so much to do. An old playpen stayed set up in the middle of the living room. "Shelley, you give the baby his bath tonight," their mother would say. "Kimmie, you heat up the bottles." After the dimness of her gramma's house, with only the light from the TV, there was too much noise and color.

From the small square window in the corner room she shared with her sister, Shelley could still see the blue faint television light ghost over the snow.

Once, Shelley's gramma said, "Why don't you go out and play with the kids your age?"

Shelley didn't think of it until later, but it was the same as Shelley saying that she should do something with the other gramma. Maybe it was natural if you loved a person to want them to have somebody besides just you.

But Shelley didn't want to. There weren't many kids her age on Keck Road. Across the street, the youngest Umber-hum was Nell, and she was years ahead, already at college. Petey was the age of her brothers. Down at the far end of the road, two kids lived in the house that was a tavern at night, but they belonged to Church of Modern Day Christ, which in those days made them seem like completely different people.

The only kid on Keck Road who was in her grade at school was Buddy Janson, a white-blond boy who wore black glasses and stayed inside all day with his fat mother. He would hide under her skirts, and he even wore skirts himself. He'd tip around in her high heels. And she just smiled, the fat mother, while this was going on. The other mothers shook their heads whenever they talked about it.

His little brother, Wesley, was the opposite, always out-side doing wheelies, even on the ice.

IV

*I*n college, Bea and June Umberhum never became close. A few times, they veered close to being close, but it never stuck.

But somehow now they were, because they both had been away. It was not only that they were from here and here again. They were *back*, they would each say, with a falling sigh meant to imply that the ends of their stories, the portion that included the startling redemption, had not yet begun.

They both lived downtown, in apartments. Bea's was on the top floor of a new building. June rented the second story of a house owned by a couple with a grown daughter, who could sometimes baby-sit Peggy.

After college, Bea had worked in Chicago as a copywriter in an advertising agency. Then, when she was twenty-seven, her mother called one week and said she couldn't peel the potatoes, her hands were so stiff. The next week, she couldn't clean herself after defecating. Rheumatoid arthritis. Even with the special treatment other doctors gave Hazel because of her husband, they determined she could no longer drive. Bea's omnipotent older sister was already married, living in Minneapolis, her first baby on the way.

Bea resigned from the agency—offering two months' notice; she felt that was enough, given the nature of her reason—and returned.

Her father was against it; weirdly, she thought.

"Come up for a visit, but whatever you do, don't quit your job, for Pete's sake. Older people get these things. Feet, fingers, teeth. She doesn't need you to live here."

For years, Bea and her mother had puzzled over the myriad details the doctor deemed unnecessary. There was very little to do with anything but acute illness that was, to his mind, necessary.

At first, Bea worked for *The Press Gazette,* reporting on the controversy surrounding the Reforestation Camp, built by inmates of the penitentiary. She also took photographs, the way she had for De Pere High's *Sentinel.* Hers was the front-page picture of the children lighting candles on the Norway spruce in front of City Hall.

This job allowed Bea time to drive her mother to her club meetings, to arrange her flowers (according to her directions; *no, the iris taller, there, a bouquet has to have height at the center*)—to do the small tasks that mattered but that the doctor could never have done. Bea followed instructions, even when they drove her crazy. Her mother was a member of the Saint Fialcra Gardeners Club, Bread and Book ("where we read and eat," Hazel explained), Doctors' Wives, and several bridge leagues.

Those first years, Bea dated a few of the boys she'd known in high school, who were also home again. At least it seemed to her mother that she dated them. She never really had a steady, not that her mother knew of, not in the way other people meant when they used that word.

Bea herself had often been unsure whether a Sunday-night excursion to the movies was an expression of romantic interest or of the more simple need for companionship.

This uncertainty made Bea's mother shake her head warily; in her day, there was no such thing as a coed excursion to the movies that was not a date. "What else could it *be*?" she'd say as they talked afterward at the kitchen table, drinking Ovaltine. Hazel always kept a store of Girl Scout cookies. She believed the girls of this generation, some of them, had let the young men get what they wanted too easily, spoiling it for everybody else.

Bea's mother had been careful to raise her with the right amount of fear, for a girl. And she'd found her intelligent daughter to be a quiet, absorbing student.

She'd had smug moments of triumph when Bea was in high school that now pained her to remember. A number of her friends had had problems with their girls.

"Boy-crazy," she'd said then, in the car, on their way home from Lil's house. It never seemed to happen that Bea was truly friends with a daughter of one of her friends, but the girls had known one another all their lives and could certainly entertain themselves together while their mothers talked downstairs.

And her mother didn't worry too much that Bea made other, different friends. Bea seemed, well, better than her friends' girls were turning out.

They were all tizzying about hair and makeup and dances. Her daughter showed the normal teenage excitements, too, but over different things. She loved sports and went cross-country skiing at night. She was active in the March of Dimes, and in 1953, she collected $428 worth of dimes, making the rounds of all the downtown shops and then bicycling out to collect from farmhouses and gas stations along the old highway. She was photographed for *The Press Gazette* with her dimes stacked up in towers; her mother sent a copy of that picture to Eleanor Roosevelt, who, eleven months later, sent one back of herself, standing with Adlai Stevenson and Franklin Jr., her signature in white ink!

Bea was always a member of one committee or the other at school, and often an officer. Before some event, a volley of phone calls would ring through the house.

But it seemed Bea needed to be given a subject. The other girls, her friends' daughters, made up their own sneaky subjects, which they wouldn't tell you, even if you asked what they were talking about. "Nothing," they always answered.

About the middle of Bea's junior year, her mother began to worry that she'd done too good a job. She hadn't wanted boy-crazy, but was it altogether natural for a girl to be so moderate?

That weekend, her tall, longhaired daughter was moping around the house in her kneesocks.

"What's the matter with you?" she'd said.

"No one wants to do anything. I wanted to go cross-country skiing, but everyone just wants to stay home. There was some dance last night and they're all tired." She shrugged her shoulders.

To Bea's mother, it was clear; the group was breaking down into couples—two and two and two.

And somehow, Bea was left alone. Bea seemed untroubled that she wasn't pairing up herself; she was only bewildered that everyone else seemed to like this new kind of game.

Perhaps she'd gotten used to groups; she was too good at being a team member.

Still, maybe it was best, Bea's mother told her husband, whom she talked to as a way of talking herself into things. Maybe the really *nice* kids didn't start in on all those shenanigans until senior year. Or even college.

College, then, it would have to be, because senior year seemed to go much as junior year had. Bea was on the girls' golf team and also served as class vice president. She organized a busful of students to ride all night to a Michigan elementary school, to help with the U.S. Public Health Service's field trials. Once there, they were put in charge of changing an ordinary playground into a clinic. They swept, hosed, and painted while nurses inoculated 291 children in the first three grades. Half were getting the real McCoy, half just some ordinary liquid. No one knew which was which. Bea and the other Wisconsin seniors mopped, folded tables, and then rode home again, singing on the bus. Bea was codirector of the decorations committee for the prom.

Still, there was something not quite normal in it, her mother sometimes feared.

Around two o'clock, day of the prom, she received a call from the beauty shop. Bea was not yet there for her appointment, and it was already sixteen after.

Well. Fortunately, Bea's mother kept a standing appointment with Rolf (bumper sticker: I'M A BEAUTICIAN, NOT A MAGICIAN) at four o'clock every Saturday. At worst, she could give her daughter that and just go in with her for the manicure.

But she drove the Oldsmobile over to the school right then and found her daughter on top of a ladder in the middle of the gym, delivering orders to two bespectacled boys who probably played violin in the orchestra. They were hanging bunched-together sheets spray-painted blue to resemble waves. The theme was deep undersea life, and Bea was apparently unsatisfied with the boys' painted renditions of white-caps. In the corner, near the door where you walked in, was an ocean-bottom treasure chest to collect dimes. That in particular unnerved Hazel. Charity was a good thing, but enough was enough. A prom was a prom.

But this was how her daughter was most herself. In her dungarees, sneakers, no makeup, long, thick hair rubber-banded. Shouting to befuddled friends who came from uncertain houses, who couldn't have ever been admitted to the top crowd.

That was what had always galled Bea's mother. Bea could've run with that crowd. Effortlessly. Why didn't she? her mother wondered, while also admiring the squarish, stylized orange goldfish her daughter had cut out and painted the previous weekend at home.

That night, as Dr. Maxwell took Bea's photo standing with Ned Phillips (just a friend, also on the decorations committee), a corsage on her wrist, her hair "done" by Rolf, feet jammed into the silver high heels her mother had selected at Kendalls, she looked like half of herself.

Those boys—the prom helpers—would have asked Bea out, but she had a way of discouraging them. She seemed not to understand their innuendos. Her demeanor with them was the same as with everyone: happy, cheerful, busy, occupied, oblivious to the whole underworld of flirtation, as if she were missing the receiving wires.

Hazel thought the boys were daunted because they never saw Bea's hands still. Now she'd taken up knitting. The home economics teacher at school taught her how. She'd read somewhere that the first person they tried the oral vaccine on, after cows and chickens, was a feeble-minded boy in a state institution. They slipped him the vaccine in chocolate milk. Bea was knitting that boy a scarf.

Another concern tagged Bea's mother that spring and summer before college, when a good deal of her time was spent on lists and labels, packing up her youngest to go away.

The weight.

Bea was not overweight by any medical measure. No, according to her father's charts, she was right on the money for her age and height; and her mother never would have said she was overweight. In fact, a few years back, she and Bea had scoffed at the ridiculous energy so many of the girls seemed to spend worrying about their bodies.

Jen's girl—a cheerleader—did a chant with her friends and then fell over giggling.

> We must,
> We must,
> We must develop the bust.
> The bigger the better,
> The tighter the sweater.
> The boys depend on us!

It was crazy. Just crazy.

Bea's mother had visited her friend Lil, whose twin girls—wraiths, practically—had just clomped in from a five-mile jog. They stood in the kitchen—polite, deferential, their clean hair soft on their shoulders—murmuring between themselves. At a cutting board, the taller sliced open a head of lettuce. She quartered it and they ate the wedges, standing there bent over.

"That'll probably be their dinner," Lil said, shaking her head.

Bea's mother had been so appalled, she had to say something. "There's nothing in that, Lil. Only water. They need protein and iron, vitamins. They're still growing."

Lil never put a real dinner on the table—Lil always worked. She gave most of the girls in their part of town, Bea included, piano lessons. She had to—since the war, her husband had been handicapped.

"But remember what *we* did?" Lil said, falling into her easy, cascading laugh. She reminded Hazel of the time they'd arranged their own Birthday Ball here in Green Bay, the night of FDR's birthday. Hazel had tied her girdle so tight that she'd fainted and they'd had to walk her to Saint Vincent's Hospital. She'd also accepted two prom invitations, one to her school, one to Catholic Boys'. They'd called it prom-trotting.

But she hadn't gone to either one, because that night, in Saint Vincent's Emergency Room, she'd met the young physician.

While the other girls were fussing, comparing breasts and ankles and every small knob of bone on their legs, Bea seemed altogether indifferent. She wrote a letter to Maurice J. Tobin, Truman's secretary of labor, on behalf of Beth Penk, their housekeeper. Beth's husband had been laid off from Nicolet Paper when a machine dislocated his shoulder. She talked her parents into raising Beth's wage. Hazel had just wanted to give Beth a little something to help with the doctor bills.

Hazel sometimes thought of her daughter's letters, in the White House, in a mailbag with hundreds of others, her daughter's collected dimes added onto a mound high as the coal piles.

And she was still knitting—leg warmers, now, which she sent to Sister Kenny's clinic in Minneapolis and the Gillette Crippled Children's Hospital. Her pièce de résistance was a cape for a beauty queen in an iron lung, an Aran-stitched X and O cable.

"Now when is she ever going to wear that?" Hazel muttered.

It was as if adolescence—that new word that everyone all of a sudden knew—was a contagion Bea somehow had not caught. She agreed with her reasonable parents. She found high heels ridiculous. She ate casseroles and desserts with the abandon of a ten-year-old boy.

And no, she wasn't overweight, her mother conceded, but neither did she have the narrow profile, with long, thin limbs poking out of sleeves, that so many of the girls did then.

It was a sign, a dance of mating, the way heels were and stockings and the square spot of purple on a female duck. A dab of makeup and the other little touches made a girl seem a normal girl, among the flock.

Inside the music.

Bea told her mother that people washed their hair more often than necessary because some businessperson had thought of a brilliant way to make more profit, off of women's heads.

"Well, we're fortunate," her mother said. "We can afford the shampoo. So go ahead and use all you like."

Her mother remembered that conversation a few years later, when Bea took the job with the advertising firm on Michigan Avenue, in Chicago.

She hoped in Chicago Bea was washing her hair.

Bea had never been truly oblivious. It would have surprised Hazel to learn that for two years of high school her daughter had considered herself to be in love with Alexander Pray, a delicate boy she could barely speak to. Her body changed when he passed by her in the school hallway. She sweated behind her knees; her mouth went dry. He was a high note. Other boys—the ones who helped her on the prom committee and followed along to meetings for the March of Dimes—hardly registered as notes at all; they were only rhythm, everyday comic noise. Burps, suction, a can opening.

Alexander went along on the overnight trip to Michigan. Right before they left, as they were packing their duffels into the hold of the bus, Bea's mother stood talking to him, alone. She lectured him, telling him that her daughter had no experience of overnight outings with young men and that she expected her back in one piece.

Sometimes, Bea knew that Alexander was out of her league. Other times, she thought it was just possible he liked her.

On that trip, they'd sat together. His arm had flung around her—or was it just resting on the top of the high bus seat? They'd slept with their heads together on the bumpy ride home.

Did anything happen or not? Could it have? To this day, Bea wasn't sure, although one night, in their forties, in a bar, Alex Pray told her about Hazel's warning.

No, Bea had kept him secret, an arrogant secret, the pure high note. Later, she was ashamed to talk about it because of how little there had been.

It had happened in Chicago, too. The head of the firm; married. He probably never knew how much she felt.

During the years her daughter was away, Bea's mother had gone with several of her girlfriends out to the ecumenical church by the college. The services there were just different—less organ music and more about people's real problems, the kinds of problems they didn't talk about themselves yet but heard talked about on TV.

There was a wonderful young priest, Father Matthew. Now that Bea was back, more stylish, if not much slimmer, her mother thought she'd have him over to dinner one night. Maybe he could help her daughter. He had grown up here. He must know people. His friends couldn't all be priests.

Not much was going on in the dating department.

Bea's mother now blamed herself. She'd done too good a job raising Bea. Half of rearing a girl was scaring her into not crossing the perilous line between popular girl and loose, sex being the line itself. The good popular girls, Bea's mother noticed, suggested sex, implied it in their movements, even in the chiming music of their voices as they ambled together in a group like a cloud. But God forbid, they knew better than to give it away, to allow their bodies to be used.

. . .

One constant: the knitting.

While she was gone, a TV show came on the air out of Milwaukee, called *The Busy Knitter.* One of the girls in Bread and Book watched and knit along with the hostess, making the Scandinavia sweater. But when the show went off the air, she was only at the underarm. She called the local station, and they said, "That's all the cans we have," and so Hazel sent the whole mess, needles and everything, to Bea in Chicago. When Bea sent it back, she'd whipped off a hat to go with.

She said she'd knit through important meetings in Chicago. But now all her yarn was black!

Since she'd been back, Bea always looked like she was going to a funeral. Black eyeglasses, black sweaters, black slacks.

Even in her late twenties, Bea was nowhere near the line. If the popular girls—or women, I suppose, her mother thought—flirted with the line, touching it and then jumping back, Bea was at the other end of the field altogether.

And now that she was back, the pond seemed still.

Maybe it was too late. Maybe they were all already married.

But then Bea began palling around with that divorced Umberhum girl, who'd also been away. And the Umberhum girl was dating, all right. Bea's mother heard she was doing quite a bit more. But she supposed that was different. She'd already been married, had a child.

Bea's mother was pretty much resigned to the idea that this so-called friend who was always slapping her own hip in her sharkskin slacks, this June, would get married again for the second time before Bea ever got her first turn. But now that Bea was almost thirty, her mother felt she couldn't say much. It was hard for Hazel to think of her daughter's virginity. Was it still a good thing?

For a first-time marriage, yes, it had to be. But not for too too much longer.

Stumped, Hazel had to take the pins out of her bun and shake her head. She always pictured a clear liquid in a jar that, shaken, revealed flakes of sediment.

In her own day, a girl like that, who'd had a husband leave his marks and shape, given birth already, was nothing a decent man would look for, in a wife.

And Bea?

Bea became good friends with the priest.

That priest who was supposed to be helping her.

But—what do you know?—it seemed Father Matthew liked to go for Chinese, too. They drove to the place a Hmong family had opened outside town, surrounded by snowy fields, Bea, June, Father Matthew, and Lord knew who else. So Bea had her group again.

"Uch," was all Bea's mother would say. She would not drive to the ecumenical center anymore.

Her friends, who were sensitive women, stopped going, too.

V

*I*n 1967, Shelley's mother explained the whole system of female sins. She illustrated them on Shelley's little brother's blackboard, just as she had with the planets and the different branches of our government. That had been hard to listen to. Shelley's attention had drifted, much like it did at school.

Sitting on their lap was a form of petting, egging them on. Letting them touch you or put their tongues in different places, your ears or arms, say, was also dangerous.

Kimmie was invited to a party at a house way out in the boonies, where there were going to be boys.

Their mother got a ragged laugh when she said, "Oh, they'll try, all right."

"Why don't you talk to them two?" Kim asked, nodding toward the room where Butch and Tim shared bunk beds. "Tell them the sins."

"They're boys." Her mother shrugged. "Plus they know."

Shelley had been in the room all the time, sitting on her bed holding her hands in her lap like two big leather mitts.

She was already taller than both of them, and strong. Recently, she'd lifted a nine-foot hickory limb felled by lightning.

"What about her?" Kim pointed.

Their mother's mouth pulled down. Maybe she was thinking of it for the first time. "Don't you let anyone fool with you, Shelley," she said quietly, but stern. "Some boy may try, but it'll only be to laugh at you for it later."

Shelley saw herself considered with a new consternation—a tooth mismatched with a lower tooth, making her mother's whole face look broken.

Shelley knew she wasn't pretty. Not from looking in the mirror; she stared at her reflection in the bathroom medicine chest door many minutes of those days, but—to herself—she looked just about like everybody else. No, she understood from how boys at school were with her and her sister. Here at home, on Keck Road, it was easier. But in school, Shelley had to do more to get their attention. She had to rush hard to be in the right place; she had to say something; she could not let up. Kimmie, she just got it all coming to her from different directions. Kimmie was the center of a star.

But her mother was still looking at Shelley, worried now.

So there was sex for the pretty and for the unpretty, too. You weren't entirely spared either way.

Shelley could tell it would be different for her than for Kimmie or for June across the street and her daughter, Peggy, whose clothes were as clean and sugary as molded Easter eggs with paper scenery inside them. With them, she thought, it would be quaint like a valentine. Precise touches, trembling, hummingbirds eating from flowers.

For Shelley, though, it would be something else, a way of catching her, getting her down to hurt her, dust in her mouth and dry heat, a rubbing.

She had seen it with animals. Once it was started, they

couldn't stop, even if people shouted, even if everyone was looking.

She'd seen dogs like that in George's yard, the one on the bottom looking out at you with big eyes when you clapped or called, hanging helpless because it needed that hit hit hit.

It was hard for Shelley to be around people her own age. Those occasions made her excited and sad, sometimes alternating, sometimes all at once.

Most of the time, she kept quiet in school and on the playground. But when she said something, it could come out wrong—a rectangular bar that stayed in the air and made people look at her acutely. That was her experience: people not looking at her at all and then full on, suddenly sharp, as if she was a danger.

It was a little better out Keck Road in her old clothes. The kids ran together down to the railroad tracks. Sometimes they shot skeets. Shelley was a straight shot, but she never got her own gun, like her brothers. And later on, different as she was, she sided, the way the other girls and women did, with the birds, that they should have a finished life, complete, just like a person, dying when they were already old, for them, in their years. Let the birds be, she said.

On that dead-end street, what the children spoke of, fought over, taunted one another with all the time was money. Funny to think of on a road with eight houses, none of them worth much, off the highway running east–west, almost out of town. The first house as you turned in was the Keck house, a small box of cream color. Then there were empty wooded lots until Dave Janson, who lived with his fat wife and two boys. At the end was the biggest yard, first cleared by Phil Umberhum, who had worked for years as a guard in the tower of the penitentiary. Now his widow lived there alone.

Once, at a picnic, his grandson Petey brought a jar of olives. People talked about those olives for years. That kind of money was what made George's family different.

The kids climbed over creeks on rocks and cement drainpipes; they built forts in trees—and all these things Shelley could do. She knew to just be quiet and wait for them to notice the work she'd done. Her grandmother had told her a long time ago, when she was a kid and came running inside because the neighbor children and her brothers and sister, too, were playing Polio and wanted to make her be it.

"Don't let 'em see that it bothers you. Go right back and say, 'Okay, I'm it.' Say that like you don't give a hoot. If they see they can get you riled up, they'll just keep piling on more."

So for years she'd played Polio. She was it.

The only place she had full relief was in her gramma's house.

There was nothing Shelley could say that her gramma would mind much, and over there she didn't get the urges she sometimes had at home and at school to sass back.

And her grandmother let her flick her foot. She'd had only a little polio—so little it seemed it was something about herself, and not the polio, that made her strange to other people. It was as if a feather had brushed her with the sharp edges of each tiny thread, so fine were its marks and traces. Only one leg from the shin down, mostly the foot. And her mouth dragged a little, too, on the left.

But while she watched TV or just did nothing, she liked to flick that foot. Everyone always said, "Stop it; you're doing it again. Stop it with the foot."

Butch, her oldest brother, used to hold his shooter. Her parents said the same to him.

"Keep your hands off of it."

Then, when Shelley was fourteen, on March 16, 1971, her grandmother died.

It was a Tuesday. Shelley came home that afternoon and walked across the yard. The only snow left was gray and porous, in drifts plowed by the side of the road. Oozy black mud showed through last year's grass. She felt, the minute she let herself in, that the house was empty.

Her gramma had had a stroke in her car, the toe of her right shoe daintily pressing down the brake pedal. On the seat next to her were two envelopes she was taking to the post office and her list—"coffee, oranges, oleo."

Shelley lifted her just the way she was into the house. By then, Shelley had already grown to be over six feet.

VI

*I*n December of her third year back, Bea received a change-of-address card from the ad agency she'd worked for in Chicago. The agency had moved to New York City, to an address on Madison Avenue!

This required a special session with June at Kaap's, where they resolved to plan a shopping spree in Milwaukee.

Bea had always wanted to live in New York City. She and June worked for hours on an appropriate card to send the woman who had been Bea's boss (bribing Peggy with dimes, one at a time, buying themselves the few minutes it took her to walk to the long cases at the front of the restaurant and select a candy).

The woman who had been Bea's boss had always liked the Green Bay side of her. At first, Bea had knitted only with her hands beneath her desk, but when the head of the firm caught her at it and complimented her garter stitches, she began to purl in the open. At her wildest, she'd stuck her hair up in a bun, with a Takuma bamboo circular needle. Her boss eventually worried, as Bea's mother had, about her personal life. "How's your weekend?" she'd say. "Having fun? Good." At the office, there was a young assistant in the art department who stopped asking Bea to lunch after their meals turned out to be, well, only lunches. Married man, the boss decided, and didn't press it.

Bea and June wrote the note to her on a Green Bay post-card that showed the bridge over the Fox River lifting up in two parts as a tall boat went through.

Congratulatory but not fawning. Jaunty—with the implication she might soon be back on board, in New York. At the same time she mailed that card, Bea posted a check for a subscription to *New York* magazine.

After that was all over and Bea stopped waiting for a reply—*No, they agreed, you don't really answer a congratulations note*—June mentioned that they had lived in New York.

"When?" Bea asked, flabbergasted. Who was *"we,"* anyway?

"With him. When we were married." June was always vague about her few years with her husband. Bea could only estimate how long they were married. She knew they had lived in Milwaukee for a while. She imagined a small aluminum house with a fenced-in yard. Now, it seemed, they had been to New York, too.

"Where did you live?"

"We lived, we lived on Madison Avenue," June said. She looked away in a vague, closing way that discouraged further questions.

Bea didn't believe her, not exactly.

Bea had the distinct impression that Madison Avenue was all businesses, not residence. The way she pictured it, it was a street lined with buildings, each a little different, each one housing an ad agency.

Because her mother was so concerned with romantics, Bea tried to forget altogether what wasn't there. But there had been flickers and glimmers that, in her solitude, passed from secrets to private shame. By now, she was willing to admit it. She was no good at love. There had been misunderstandings. But she was sure that if she'd told her mother about them, they would've seemed even worse. Mysteries. Perhaps even tragedy, or crime.

There had been an all-day outing with a young college professor, new to town from Saint Paul. He'd talked about his girlfriend, an elementary school teacher still back in Minnesota. He said he was waiting for the right time to "let her down."

Only at the end, he'd told Bea the real reason: Gigi, a half-wit who worked in her father's store, attached to the filling station outside Suamico. He'd taken Bea's hand and looked her in the eyes, then asked, "What do *you* think I should do?"

She couldn't remember anymore what she'd answered.

She told the story to June at Kaap's that December night, three years after it happened. Bea's double-pointed knitting needles chittered while they talked. She was using eight-ounce alpaca, dark gray.

June cleared away the shame with her answer. "The cad," she said. "But he was interested. Definitely. That was his way of feeling *you* out."

Telling June was like an excavation. An event.

June now was working as a teacher in the Brown County school system, and they began to share the gossip they learned at their respective jobs, breaking the rumors down to their component parts. They dissected troubled marriages with particular relish.

Bea's mother, who spent a good portion of her day on the telephone or at the bridge table, could sometimes contribute. They often met at her house in De Pere and Mrs. Maxwell would join in until her bedtime, which was only a little later than Peggy's.

June was always polite to Hazel. She asked her about bridge.

"I've played since 1927. I'm still no expert. I have no master points. If I get too good, I've got nobody to play with."

The two younger women felt that they could *see* Green Bay society, the way they could in fact see Green Bay topographically from Dr. and Mrs. Maxwell's front window, which offered a clear wide view of the river, with its beauty and barges, its columns of smoke and piles of sulfur and coal.

They shared an interest in fashion. When Bea got around to something, she would dig to the bottom of the subject. And clothes no longer daunted her. She had her own style, which required trips to Milwaukee and Chicago and packages arriving from stores in places like Dallas. If she saw a dress in a magazine, she'd just order it right then. Some worked; some needed to be returned, airmail. This at an age long after most women in Green Bay had given up on such things and gotten what Hazel's hairdresser, Rolf, called "mothercuts," and perms for ease.

Hazel had always admired her daughter's thoroughness, up to a point. But there was also something to looking fresh and cleverly stylish as a young woman, when it mattered. Later on, when you were married and had children, what did you care if your clothes weren't the latest?

Hazel's arthritis came and went. Some days, she felt like an invalid; on others her old self. The day after Bea replied to the change-of-address card, her mother was in bed again, so she went to the *Press Gazette* office and quit. She walked from there to the old courthouse, where Bill Alberts worked, and asked for a job. Once before, she'd asked him for a charity donation and he'd written her a large check. "How many dimes go into five hundred dollars?" he'd said.

Bill Alberts ran the biggest real estate company in town—with his left hand, as he liked to say. People said he was the first person in northern Wisconsin to understand the meaning of land. It was Bea's idea that as a real estate agent, she could spend more time with her mother. She could even take her along.

"Edith, put Miss Maxwell on the payroll," he shouted, from his desk, into the adjoining anteroom. "Sit down, sit down," he told her.

"Today? But I haven't even started the course to get my license."

He waved away her concern, then folded his hands and looked at her directly. "So tell me your plans. Will you stay in Green Bay?"

"Oh, I think so," she said. "I've been back now—what? Three years."

"I ask because we're the generation who will bring culture home to us. Green Bay, right here." He talked quite a bit with his hands. "Our parents all drove to Chicago or at least Milwaukee to hear music, see theater, shop, whatever they did." His hands chopped and flew.

Bea tried to think if her parents ever went to Milwaukee. They had not. Once, her mother's friend Lil got up a group to drive to Goshen, Indiana, to hear Marian Anderson sing. It was the old story. At the last minute, a child was born eight weeks early and Dr. Maxwell couldn't go. Hazel had gone anyway, but she'd had a bad time. She felt conspicuous because it was three other couples and her.

Bill Alberts wore a white shirt with French cuffs and suspenders. From his phonograph speakers, a man's low, raspy voice was half-singing, half-whispering things that might better be said in private. "But we'll change all that. My sisters moved away. Every one to a bigger city. Your sister's where? Minneapolis. You see, I want to bring the cities to us here."

Bill Alberts was someone Bea could've known growing up, but she just hadn't. He was older, in the same world as her parents but Jewish. Her father worked with his parents at the hospital. He apparently had known about her, though. He'd seen her picture in the paper, he said, at the Winter Ball, ice-skating on the frozen Fox River.

That would have been along with other girls from De Pere High, she reminded him. She knew the picture. They'd worn flared felt skirts and carried fur muffs.

"I don't remember others," he said.

He was not like Alexander Pray or any of his successors, all of whom looked, one way or another, the same.

He, too, had grown up in a large house by the river. He, too, had gone away to college and then come back. Bea wasn't sure how old he was. Older, definitely. But ten years or twenty? He was a man who probably had never been handsome, so it was hard to tell. He was short, five two or five three. He'd lost the majority of his hair long ago, certainly before Bea paid him any attention, eliminating some of the usual suspense of middle age. His baldness gave a certain nakedness to his features, so that no matter what angle you beheld him from, it was hard to see him as good-looking.

His hands were always moving, making fists or baskets in midair, his fingers snapping or drumming on the desktop. Dark against the cuffs, his wrists and hands were attractive.

Bea walked to her car, holding her keys out in front, with a light step.

She felt something—a yes-and-no feeling. Not like *the* something, but something else, new, an agitation like the scratchiness of wool in spring.

She found out that evening from her mother that Bill Alberts had been a bachelor in Green Bay for many years. He'd lived with his parents. Even after he finally bought his own place—the Kaap river mansion—he went home every night to his mother's table for supper.

"Until he married *her*," Hazel said.

Some years ago, Bill Alberts had married Marge Garsh, a local girl, the undertaker's daughter. "And I suppose then *she* cooked."

From the church, Bea's mother knew the lady who had been his childhood nanny. The old woman still went to iron his shirts every Tuesday and Thursday, but she wouldn't do a thing for the wife. "Doesn't like her," Bea's mother said, as if that made perfect sense.

Money had never been a problem for the Alberts family. His father was chief surgeon at the hospital and his mother was a doctor, too, an obstetrician. That would have been unusual, even scandalous, for a woman in her time in Green Bay to have four children and keep working—except that they were Jewish. All they did was held to be in another category.

Bill Alberts himself had already made several other fortunes—ruining the city, his own father said. Bea's mother repeated that with a down-curved voice that contained a certain relish.

Bill's taste differed from his European parents', that was for sure. He had a sharp, flat American vision. Tract houses did not offend him, Bea knew, and his developments from the fifties were made of sound materials and planted with young trees. She golfed in a club that ended at the backyards of one of his subdivisions. They were cheerful houses, hard to tell whether rich or poor, and though small, they were somehow smart.

Thirty-five years later, when those trees were mature, most of the houses were still standing and in good repair.

But he didn't like to think of himself as a realtor. Everyone knew his passion was jazz music. In the thirties, some of the Big Bands had played Green Bay at the Ace of Spades, and apparently Bill's parents—the two doctors—had gone dancing. He himself played drums. For years, he'd bored anyone who would listen to his stories about trips to Chicago in the forties and fifties to hear the great bands at their peak. He'd bought himself a whole building downtown, the old Green Giant canning factory, to turn into a nightclub for his band.

Most evenings, he smoked a cigar in his office, music playing out the open windows: Buddy Rich, Gene Krupa, Jo Jones. At seven, he headed to dinner at a restaurant downtown before his own local band convened. They called themselves the Fox River Trotters. They all called him Little Jazz.

Rumor had it that there was no family life inside the stone house Bill Alberts owned on one of Green Bay's oldest and best streets. It had been the carefully tended home of the Kaaps, an elderly brother and sister who lived together for more than forty years and walked on the river path every afternoon at four.

"He runs around," Mrs. Maxwell said.

"Really?"

"I think so, sure. Yes."

But though they believed he was an unfaithful husband, Mrs. Maxwell and her friends were not sympathetic to Bill's wife. They said it was because Marge had let old Mabel Kaap's rose garden go to rack and ruin. *Thank God she's not here to see it.*

"They say Marge doesn't like music," Bea's mother said. "And you know him."

But it wasn't the roses, Bea understood, or music. Even though she'd grown up in De Pere and attended the same schools and the same church, Marge Garsh's father was the undertaker. She was a perfectly decent choice for Bill Alberts—she'd been a moderately popular girl, a candy striper in the hospital and then a cheerleader—even though she was so much younger. It was not as if he'd married someone Polish.

Still, Marge Garsh was not immune to criticism from these women, as their own daughters were, as Bea knew herself to be. When Celia Howard, a daughter of the family who owned *The Press Gazette* and one of the paper mills, lost Kip Dannenford's grandmother's pink diamond swimming in Fish Creek, Bea's mother and all her friends just laughed.

VII

One afternoon in 1970, Bea rushed into the office after a showing, before a five o'clock tee time, to write up the multiple offers that were due to come in over the next hour, when her boss summoned her to his big office.

She sat where she had the day he hired her, on the other side of his immense desk.

He looked at her in his intent way, his fingertips barely touching. "So are you still liking it here?" he asked.

"Oh, sure."

"Good," he said, musing on something. "Good." Piano music was playing in the background, but like no piano music Bea had ever heard. It was "Für Elise" spilled in a mess all over the air.

"Earning enough?"

"Well . . . " She laughed, feeling a certain discomfort in her wool suit. The breeze from the open window was watery, warm. He knew as well as she did that she'd sold seventeen houses since the first of the year, and as likely as not, he also knew the contents of her trust account at the bank.

"Of course, your sales record is excellent. If you need a larger monthly floor, expenses, whatever . . . " He waved his hands. "You know, I always tell Marge, if I were ever to leave her for someone, it would be Bea Maxwell."

"What is this?" she said.

He stood up and started to dance! "Joe Mooney, the world's only hip organ/accordian player," he said.

"We took our honeymoon in Miami because he had a regular gig at a steak house there and never played Chicago. This is 'I Wonder What Became of Me?' written in 1946 by Johnny Mercer and Harold Arlen for their Broadway flop, *St. Louis Woman.*"

She thought it was wonderful he could remember all that. His door was open. She looked instantly, her head snapping, but Edith, his tireless secretary, was not at her desk. It was a spring Tuesday, almost evening. Edith sang in the Episcopal church choir and Tuesday was practice night.

Every day, she wrote another saying on her blackboard. Today, Tuesday, April 21, 1970, it was: *Smile. It takes 72 muscles to frown, only 14 to smile.*

Dogwood branches ticked against the Federal windows, the sky outside banded with orange and peach. "They pour champagne just like it was rain," the lyrics went. "It's a sight to see, but I wonder what's become of me."

People said the paper mill's pollution was what made their sunsets so beautiful over the Fox River. Sometimes they could smell the sulfur, but not tonight. She could see the piles of black coal and yellow sulfur, two stories high.

He danced her around a bit. "He was blind, very angular. A blind man without sunglasses. Very delicate organist. He played a nightclub in New York in '63, '64. The Most, the place was called. He had his Cocktail Combo. Should have gone. Now he's in Miami again, working local clubs and playing organ in church every Sunday morning."

That old elusive happiness. Bea made some sort of motion with her arm, standing up as if she were brushing crumbs from her suit. She walked to her office then, briskly, where the phone would ring soon, and he followed her. She was aware of her calves in nylons and one-inch heels. They were being watched, moving.

There was a kiss or almost, something between a bump and a kiss. She pushed her mouth down against his jacket. She tasted wool, the scent of tobacco, noticed the sunset playing out behind the smokestacks of Fort Howard, the paper mill on the river.

The phone at last was ringing and she could untangle herself to answer.

That day was more than thirty years ago now, but Bea remembers it exactly, as a specific declension of spring.

When June Umberhum came over to the house that night, Bea didn't speak of the incident. She wanted to wait until her mother went to bed, but she did work the conversation around to the subject of the Albertses' marriage.

"He runs around," her mother said again.

"So they say," Bea challenged. "Or *you've* said."

"Oh, he does," her mother said. "I know from Mimi Platt."

"I don't blame him," June said.

"No," Mrs. Maxwell agreed.

"He's still not bad, even without the hair," June said. "But she's just a drudge. She really let herself go."

"A nothing," Mrs. Maxwell added.

"They did have the four children in—what was it, five years?" Bea mentioned.

"And that's a mistake I made, too. Boy, I wouldn't do that again," June said. "Be all for the child and nothing for the man. He wanted to go out, but I said, 'No. When I leave, she cries.' Next time, I'd let her cry."

Peggy looked up from her book, and then there was a silence. June's husband had left when Peggy was still a baby. Now she was eleven years old, sitting at Mrs. Maxwell's dining room table, doing her homework.

Slowly, the women's talk resumed, a circular rambling Bea wouldn't have had as a teenager, about hair and weight and clothes. These things were all analyzed as means, techniques toward a greater end. They wanted to talk about love, but that was harder; neither of them really knew how, though sometimes they found themselves there by accident.

All along, there was the sound of Bea's needles. She was knitting a moss-stitch throw for one of her buyers. Whenever she sold a house, she presented the new owners a "new home" throw with a label reading *A Bea Maxwell Design.* She used wool she had to send away to Italy for. She'd graduated from black to deep brown, a natural-looking uneven kid mohair and lamb's wool blend that went from thinner to thick within the same skein. She imagined priests wearing cassocks made from it, roaming the ancient evening streets of Assisi, continuing long, meandering conversations. Father Matthew had found the vendor for her in an ecclesiastical supply catalog. She made coverlets for weddings, throws for house closings, and frocks with elaborate tiny shell buttons for newborns.

Hazel thought even dark brown was a little grim for

newlyweds and infants, and more than once she suggested a pale yellow, available all over, right here.

They were students of marriage, in all its particulars. They still believed in the ideal, each of them, without saying so, but they also enjoyed their running count of the shams and disharmonies they observed around them in Green Bay homes. That was one thing that June had given Bea: a firm conviction that there were hundreds, maybe thousands, of marriages that she would not for anything in the world want to be inside.

They also discussed the small slights and bafflements each of them endured during their working day. June had paid an after-school visit to one of Peggy's classmates, whose mother had invited them to stop by for some cold turkey sandwiches. They'd arrived at 4:30 and she'd let them sit and sit, offering no refreshment. What had become of those cold turkey sandwiches?

They talked next about dyeing their hair. The other kindergarten teacher in June's school had done it—put in a rinse at home—and June had been against it and told her so, but well, now she had to admit it looked great. And so natural that you wouldn't really know. They discussed how you would do a thing like that here, though. Unless you moved.

Hazel continued shaking her head. "I wouldn't do it. Somebody's going to let the cat out of the bag, and then where will you be?"

"They say if you change the cut, too—not just the color— and if you start wearing new makeup at the same time . . ."

"But what if you get involved with somebody? Would you tell *him*?"

They both agreed they probably wouldn't.

"Well, but then what if he's in a bar some night and some schlub turns to him and says, What do you think about June Umberhum's *new* hair?"

"Try and get out of that one," Hazel said. "That I'd like to see."

"Now curls—even a permanent—that's different," June said. "It's fun."

"Like in 'Which twin has the Toni?'" Bea added. "You sort of laugh with the one who gets caught in the rain."

Hearing her mother and Bea Maxwell go on like this, Peggy ran from the dining room and flung herself on a guest bed, belly-down, to lose herself in *Nancy Drew and the Mystery of the Double Doors*, a story with a soothing, orderly formula and a crime to solve. The households in these books ran ticking in the background with a calm, even regularity. They were only what they were: background. That's what she wanted hers to be, but it wouldn't recede. Her mother was now talking about them rooming with this Bea. Peggy hated her.

June sighed. "Maybe blondes really do have more fun."

Dr. Maxwell had already retired to the bedroom, where he read the paper and waited for the nightly news. He followed the Vietnam casualties the way he'd once turned on the television to get the polio tallies every night.

At nine o'clock, Bea took her mother upstairs to her room while June tucked Peggy under the guest-bed covers (she'd fallen asleep, the book in her hands) so their conversation could continue. Their favorite thing to talk about alone was family, although they saved the subject, taking it out only after a long warm-up on people who were not central, more amusing and less dangerous. When they did talk about Bea's sister or June's brother, their voices hushed. Their siblings were each guilty of the worst crime: they were each, unfairly, their mother's favorites.

They did nothing to help. Bea's popular sister rarely even phoned her parents, and June's brother did precious little, even living right next door, but they had all the props Green Bay mothers wanted: Marriage. Children. And houses.

When Bea's sister called and Bea mentioned how glad she was because it had been so long since they'd heard from her (she kept a running count: four weeks one time, six another; the longest so far was nine), her mother quickly mentioned how busy Elaine was. And when Elaine did phone, it was usually to talk about home decoration. Her last phone call, Bea remembered, had been forty minutes all about lamps. The day Elaine and her brood drove in from Minnesota for the holidays, Bea worked late and met June at Kaap's for supper to remind herself there was another world. Her nieces, naturally, had been given her own bedroom in the house and were probably right then sifting through her belongings. Breaking them.

Near the end of their late-night discussion, Bea and June meandered to the big dry-sinked kitchen, where Bea concocted hot-fudge sundaes.

"No matter what I do or how many considerations—I mean, to the doctor, the physical therapist for the hip, I'm driving across town every week to get the rolls she likes—all I hear is the kids this and Elaine that. And Elaine doesn't do diddly-squat."

"My mother blames me for the divorce," June said, pulling her knees up close to her on the kitchen chair. "I said, 'Ma, he left me.' But she thinks I should've kept him. If I'd been easier to live with. George told her once that I sleep in an ugly position. She says to me, 'Look at Nance. If he wants to go up north, they just pick up and go.'"

Bea considered mentioning the odd chase she'd had with her boss at work. But she didn't. For some reason, she wanted to hoard it, alone.

Partly, she was ashamed; partly, she was proud. *That old elusive happiness.*

She believed her refusal was smart, a coin in her hand. She felt better afterward. There was a power in denial. Her mother had taught her that *no* was a magic word, generative: It created more and greater tries. *He'll ask again,* she thought. They all knew what they were supposed to do. They'd all been taught the same things. But June had fallen off. She may not understand.

If it had been a weekend, June might have stayed even longer, sleeping in the guest bedroom across the hall from her daughter. But it was a Tuesday. Tomorrow, she had work and Peggy had school.

Bea didn't consider until years later why it was that their almost nightly visits took place in her mother's big house, where she herself stayed over several times a week. She'd always assumed it was because of her mother. But what about Peggy?

At the end of that night, June carried the long sleeping girl out over the lawn into the backseat of her Volkswagen. Bea ran behind carrying Peggy's shoes.

VIII

When Bea was named broker of the year, in 1971, everyone gathered in her office at four o'clock to open the champagne and drink it out of Styrofoam cups, and Bill Alberts noticed the old change-of-address card on her bulletin board as the other brokers were leaving. Their efforts at festivity wore out quickly; after birthday celebrations, they were all back at their desks, cake eaten, within twenty minutes.

He looked up at her oddly. "Should we run away together to New York? We could catch Bill Evans playing the Village Vanguard."

He extracted her flexible needles from her hands, crushed her fists into his, and nicked her shoes with his into a fox-trot, singing, "'So let's keep dancing. Just bring on the news and have a ball. If that's all. There is.'"

Later on, when she looked back over her life, Bea would see that afternoon as a last chance. True, it was a joke of a question. True, he was still married, but what shimmered for her behind the lightness was something possible, dark and strange. But she hadn't lifted her head. Her mother was still alive—here in Green Bay—and infirm.

Besides, by then Bea was used to him. He no longer upset her sense of balance. Her mother, whom she'd finally told about his compliments, suggested that Bill Alberts chose her only because he knew she had too much sense ever to acquiesce. Bea wasn't sure she agreed. Though she didn't want to assume otherwise and be the fool. But inwardly, she really did believe it was she herself who excited him.

And with him, Bea adopted an exaggerated attitude of shock.

She was half-convinced that if she said, Okay, Bill, take your pants off, let's go to a hotel, he would faint on the spot.

But only half-convinced.

"Well, what about bringing culture to Green Bay?" she finally answered him.

"Changed my mind," he said, walking out shaking his head. "You know Marge and the kids moved to a house in Ashwaubenon."

Bea did know that, of course. Everyone did. And what a house! Seven bedrooms. People said there were "built-in" saunas in three of the baths.

He sighed. "Someday, Bea Maxwell, you're going to wish you'd taken me seriously."

One thing she did think that turned out to be wrong: She'd counted on him making his half-joke propositions to her forever.

A year later, Bill Alberts was pursuing June.

He wouldn't have dared when she was in high school or home for vacation from college. Even being from where she was from, June had been prom queen of Prebble High and sorority sweetheart. In her mind, at least, she didn't need to make any compromises.

But being back, living in a rented top of a house with a daughter, on her own—that carried a certain air of defeat that made her approachable.

And she did join him for weekend lunches. She invited him along on Sunday-afternoon forays with Peggy and Bea and Father Matthew. At that time, while she was working for the Brown County school district, June was planning to open a flower store. Weekends, she led the whole group (Peggy often brought along a friend) into the woods, where she foraged, bringing back branches, leaves, pussy willows, cattails and pinecones. She mixed these up with the flowers she bought sparingly, arranging them in vases on the floor.

Bill thought June showed a great talent. He hired her to do a weekly arrangement for the real estate office. It was set on the front table, as you walked in, with a little card that said *Flowers by June Umberhum.*

One day, he stopped by Bea's office. She was working on a mortgage, phone to ear, wearing golf clothes, knitting. He stood in her doorway and said, "You know, I go to see a psychiatrist. And for years, every time I lay on that couch, I heard a strange sound. Like little bones snapping. And finally then, you walked into my office one day with your needles and black yarn and I knew what it was. I told her, I said, 'Dr. Klicka, you're knitting on my time.'"

"And?" Bea said.

"She wasn't the least bit apologetic. She said Anna Freud knit."

June went along as his date to the opening of his River-club, which he hoped would put Green Bay on musicians' touring circuits. Billy Eckstine played. Bill had recruited him after he'd heard him perform at the Holiday Inn in Milwaukee. "Nobody wants crooners anymore," Bill said on a Wednesday afternoon in the office. "And he was a big star in the forties and fifties." The party was on the top story of the old canning factory, overlooking the river, their Fox River, which required darkness and scattered light to achieve any romance and to obscure its mounds of coal and sulfur and the smokestacks of the paper mills.

But the next evening, returning the knit black cashmere shawl and evening bag she'd borrowed, June lingered in the Maxwells' living room, to describe the event. In front of Bea, Dr. and Mrs. Maxwell, and Peggy, June did barefoot imitations of Bill—his crooked walk, coattails flapping. He was a short man, so, giving her performance, June bent her knees. She copied how he played the drums at the end of the opening-night party, his tongue going outside his mouth, his face contorting. She was a good mimic: Everyone laughed except Bea and her father, who stood up and left the room, saying, "Leave the poor man be."

"He had pictures of Jewish jazz drummers framed behind the bar," June said, "and one of Vince Lombardi. He said that was for the hoi polloi. It was the only one I recognized. Get with the *times,* I wanted to say." Then she hummed a little something from "Let It Be."

Bea's hands shook. Bill Alberts had told her that there were an inordinate number of great Jewish jazz drummers. It seemed to be his only source of pride in his heritage.

"And authors, too," Bea had told him.

By now, Bea knew the names in his pantheon. Buddy Rich, Tiny Kahn, Stan Levey, Mel Lewis, Shelly Manne, Jack Sperling, Saul Gubin, and Dave Tough. He'd played her cuts of each of their hits. She especially remembered Saul Gubin, who'd recorded sound tracks in Hollywood studios.

"Well, you don't *sound* in love with him," Mrs. Maxwell said.

"I don't even know what love is anymore." June sighed. "At my age."

"You're not!" Peggy shouted from the kitchen table, where she'd retreated with her schoolbooks. "He's a boob."

Mrs. Maxwell concurred. "No. Trust me, dear. You are not."

Bea hadn't said anything. She didn't want June to take him—it was a definite, stabbing feeling. She didn't know why.

That was 1972. They were each thirty-five years old.

After he stopped trying—"a little soon, if you ask me," June said. "I mean, if you really want something, and he did, I could tell, then go for it a little"—the two women went out one windy, wet, warm spring day and bought silver services at Bakes. Bea couldn't admit she'd felt the same way, because she'd never really come out and told June he'd chased her, too. And now that it was over, she wished she had. It was a relief to be like June in this. Relief, at this age, almost equaled triumph.

Not wanting to at first, but finally joking it was maybe inevitable, each selected the same pattern: the Normandy Rose. It was the most elegant. Bea just wrote a check, and June bought hers on time.

It was a small step. A small step to settlement in this life.

The old man at Bakes remembered Bea from her March of Dimes campaign. "I still keep a jar," he said, showing her a small urn on the counter.

They felt the regular measure of Peggy, who seemed to be growing up so much faster than they were. And her own life now, most of it, had been lived in this town.

Bea was elected to join her mother on the board of the historical society, called Heritage Hill. She joined the club to find pickup games of golf.

June read an article in *Life* about an East Coast wedding on Cape Cod. The caption said that baby lobsters—called crawdaddies by the locals, it noted in parentheses—were flown in from eastern Wisconsin. *Eastern Wisconsin? That's here!*

So she started asking around. And sure enough, outside of town—farther out than Keck Road, where June's mother and brother still lived—there were bars that on Friday nights served crawdaddies in baskets with your beer.

They drove past the dammed banks of the Fox River on the east side, where the water was filled with bobbing logs ten to twenty feet long.

"That'll all be paper," Bea said. Whenever she could, she'd offer Peggy, in the backseat, bits of information. She'd noticed that June's instructions were mostly improvements Peggy could make—to her behavior, her posture, her hair.

Parked in front of the first bar, Bea was paralyzed by the powerful desire to stay put. Peggy was scrunched up, reading by the tiny car light in the backseat. "This doesn't look so good, June. With Peggy?"

She knew Peggy was June's daughter, but she was with her a lot, too. Once or twice, she'd silently considered teaching Peggy to knit. She was waiting for the right opening to bring it up.

"Well, we're here," June said. "We might as well try it. People are flying them in dry ice all the way to Massachusetts.

If we've got to live here, we might as well get what's best of it!"

The first bar didn't have any, but, from the bartender, they got directions to more distant and shabbier places, down close to the river. In the shack where they finally found the crawdaddies—they were called crayfish by *these* locals—it was all men except for one decrepit old woman in the corner, stationed in an armchair under the TV.

But the men were eating baby lobsters, all right. June and Bea and Peggy—with a soda pop Bea had bought her—sat on bar stools, the briny juice tickling as it dripped down their arms, under their sleeves, to the elbows.

On the way home, they drove to June's mother's to drop Peggy. June did that sometimes, when she needed to get school reports done or had a date or just needed to let off some steam and be alone.

Tonight she had a stack of student dictations that needed to be typed and pasted on construction paper. The question she and the other teacher had asked the kindergarteners was, "If I had one hundred dollars, I would buy . . . " More than one child had answered, "I'd buy my mother a house."

"You should almost use that to advertise," June said. Bea still thought of jingles sometimes, and she tried to use them on her flyers. But her work was boring her lately. "Or best offer" was a joke she shared with Bill.

But Peggy didn't want to go to her grandmother's.

"I have homework," she whined. "Two tests on Monday."

"Do it there," June said. "I always did."

"But she goes to bed so early."

"You can stay up. I'll tell her you have to study."

This part of town had been incorporated into Green Bay

proper in 1964. Much of the land off 141, which had been wooded the first time Bea saw it, was beginning to be developed. Fields, with silos in the distance, were marked out with one road, pastel small houses budded on either side.

"It's all getting built-up over here, too," June said.

"I should really drive out one day and take a look around." This was now part of Bea's profession. For families just starting out, these properties would be more affordable. She'd done well so far by selling the large homes of her mother's friends, but this was newer, more compelling. It meant more, even though the commissions would be smaller. Besides, Bea was sick of beautiful houses.

Maybe everything was that way in sales. Bea knew old Mr. Campbell, the main decorator in town. They'd meet every few months, at Bosses. "These people tear out a picture from a magazine," he told her, "and say, 'I want it to look like this.' All for four thousand dollars. 'Well, I can make it look like that,' I tell them, 'if you let *me* take the pictures.'"

Beauty had begun to seem a sham. And it meant so much to her mother. Hazel could sit at tea in her breakfast room and talk for an hour about a shade of green. There was a door they always passed on a riverside, Dutch-roofed house, an old door from the last century. The owners had painted it a pretty color, somewhere between China red and the shade of a bittersweet berry. Her mother, if left alone, would comment on that every time they passed. Every single time.

What they all wanted, hankering after a life that looked like a picture, was permanence. Whereas Bea and Mr. Campbell understood that it was all a performance, with its opening night, its run and closing. Anyone with half a mind to see reality would notice the amount of peak-open flowers in those magazine spreads.

And Bea remembered her mother's letdowns and subdued rages, after a big party, after Christmas, when her energy was spent and her bones felt hollow.

Of course, in a few weeks, a month, it would start all over again. Even in the dead of winter, Hazel and her friends made expeditions to some nursery forty miles away, where one of them had heard they had the best narcissus bulbs.

"Why?" Bea would sometimes wonder. Her mother would only shrug. "There's only so much bridge you can play."

Bea had often wished she could teach her mother to knit, but—the arthritis.

Keck Road—where she was turning now—had at first been paved in only as far as the original four houses. By the time June finally brought Bea home, there were eight. No more homes had been built since then, but there was big talk. The fields, owned by the two large nurseries, had always grown alfalfa, strawberries, and cow corn. In summer, they hired the local children. Once, when she was small, Peggy had wanted to pick strawberries, June said. But there was nothing pastoral about it. Her fingers bled and she'd gotten a sunburned nose and quit before the end of the day. Her mother, frosting on moisture cream, had scolded her for doing it at all. They paid twenty-six cents a flat.

Now one of the nurseries was buying out the other. Bill Alberts was brokering the transaction. But he was doing less of the fine work—busy with the Riverclub and the Fox River Trotters. By now, he'd named his ballroom More, after the one in New York called The Most. Bea would ask him to let her work with the developers, to pick out good stoves, simple sinks, and floors. People wanted carpet, but flooring lasted longer. That was one reason she liked her dark yarns.

"The Garshes used to live out here," June said, "over there, in that place. And then when Marge was nine or ten, they bought the smallest little house in De Pere." Her voice curved, scolding around her point. She was still bitter about Keck Road. "And then Marge was in with all those kids."

Bea was one of those kids. Or if she was not one of them, she'd known them all her life, graduated with them from Miss Pimm's Nursery Day and, for that matter, De Pere High. She looked down at her hands on the steering wheel.

Marge Garsh was the now-estranged wife of Bill Alberts, the one who had let herself become a drudge.

Well, that's what this neighborhood was, all right, Bea thought, people who weren't about to buy the smallest house in De Pere so their daughters could get in with any crowd. "But you wouldn't have married Bill Alberts," she murmured.

June sighed. "Maybe I should've. Who knows."

Had she seriously considered him? Had he made an offer? "What have they done over there?" Bea asked, changing the subject.

They were passing June's brother's place. It was late spring, and George's front yard looked ominous, a building site in the dark. There was a hauling truck and a pile of dirt more than twenty feet high.

"Oh, he built his own swimming pool. Yah. With that little Shelley across the street. They all say she's a good worker. Better than the boys. Now I think they're putting in a Jacuzzi."

Peggy didn't know Shelley anymore. She was too old to need a baby-sitter now when she was at her grandmother's, and she didn't go outside to play there either; she had homework. She was already concerned about her score on the PSAT, a test she doubted the kids on Keck Road had even heard of or would ever take.

IX

When Shelley's grandmother died in 1971, George Umberhum went to the funeral. Just him, not any of the rest of the family—not his wife, not his son. Not his mother, the other grandmother Shelley had wanted to make into her gramma's friend so long ago, though she'd lived across the street from her for all those years. Certainly June didn't go. Not even the Kecks. The fat woman sent over a casserole. Her son Buddy, now a high school sissy, delivered it covered with a dish towel.

At the funeral, George talked about his latest dream: He wanted to build a swimming pool in his yard, that summer.

Even before school was out, he had Shelley working every day with him to dig the hole.

The summer before, Shelley had picked for the nurseries. Almost every kid on Keck Road had tried one time or another, but most left after a few hours of midday sun, their fingers swollen and bleeding. None of the Umberhum kids had done it; they got better jobs. The Umberhum girls were legendary anyway, but older. Their father had been a prison guard, but the girls were all pretty and smart, and won scholarships to college. The only kid who didn't go was George. And his son,

Petey, didn't have to work summers. He just rode his bike to the park every day and played Ping-Pong.

By July, the year before, only Shelley and two of her brothers were still picking. At the end of that summer, the nursery had hired Shelley's brother Tim to work year-round in their store. They couldn't take Shelley because of the way she looked. It was a job serving the public. They told her as much and expected her to understand.

So by the time George Umberhum hired her, she was doing yard work for all the neighbors. She raked and mowed lawns, shoveled and plowed in winter. When the mower or plow broke, she knew how to replace a belt or change the filter.

She does a nice job with the yard, they said about her.

The women shook their heads. *If it weren't for that leg.*

George had a vision of what he wanted. He'd seen places, on vacation down in Florida and up in the Peninsula, where he and Nance sometimes went camping.

He never before had built anything bigger than a model of the B-52, the Flying Fortress bomber. He sent away for brochures, and he and Shelley studied the possibilities that spring in the breezeway. There were different sorts of materials and shapes and sizes: rectangle, oval, kidney, L-shaped. Before they started, he checked out a stack of books from the library, written twenty and thirty years before, published in Florida and California. These showed pictures of families in out-of-date clothes gathered around their pools having luau parties.

In May, they marked the site with chalk and began. They dug dirt out onto tarps and then dragged the tarps around the house to the front yard. Altogether, they moved more than 170 tons of dirt.

"Oh, it's all real glamorous to her," Shelley's mother said.

Working together every day, George and Shelley got to talking about almost anything they thought of, even about going to the bathroom and the problem of gas. Just because of the boredom of digging, Shelley knew everything.

Nance didn't let him touch her *there*.

At first, way back when they were young, she'd told him it was because it tickled. For a while, he believed that. He even wrote away to a magazine to ask advice.

"And what did they tell ya?" Shelley asked.

"Don't remember anymore. Couldn'ta been much."

Later on, Nance said she just didn't like it.

"She thinks *she's* holding on to the royal jewels," he said. "Well, she can keep 'em. More like a fruit basket gone bad."

Whenever her name came up, Shelley's mother always said Nance had been very very pretty when she was young.

"Maybe her mother told her not to," Shelley suggested.

"Nance's ma? Naw. I'm sure she never mentioned a thing about sex."

There. There it was. The word. Sex for the pretty and the unpretty. Shelley supposed they'd had sex for the pretty.

He told her about what he'd done in the war. They were stuck on an island where there were women who looked like a breed between regular boys and ponies, women with manes, who didn't wear tops. And they let George and the other guys do all kinds of stuff to them, things he described, softly laughing.

She shook her head. "I don't think that way even about animals."

He looked up, penitent, young-seeming, even sweet. He waited a minute, as if this was something he'd never thought

about before but now had to. "Well, they couldn't even talk—
English, I mean. They had their own language, I s'pose."

And what they then began was something there was no
name for.

Shelley started it. She was the one. They were working on
a June day. They'd poured the concrete already and were set-
ting in the tiles. It was hard to keep them at right angles.

"Hey, you over there, I've got an itch," she said. She knew
she could act that way with him, she didn't know why. She was
testing. The gate was always there for her to open. It was a
delicious feeling, icy, and, like ice, it contained shock.

She thought it was probably what normal girls had all
the time, with high school boys, even ones they liked.
With her sister, Kimmie, she could tell. Kimmie bossed her
boyfriend.

Shelley's itch got him coming over to where she was. He
had a big gut he tried to carry around daintily; it spilled over
his shorts, but he was delicate on his long, thin legs. Nance
would look at Shelley dragging her foot, then at him, and say,
"It would have to be a boy to get those legs."

It wasn't really warm yet; there was still a taste of cold
dark water in the air, but they were both hot from work.

And there was a smell of rot you could feel in your teeth.
Spring out where they lived reeked. The snow melted slowly,
unless they had a big rain. It just got gray and dirt-pocked,
and Shelley imagined all the piles of animal make that were
released now, into the air, moist and thawed.

Her legs were stretched out in the sun on the concrete of
what was going to be the pool.

Our pool, he always said. Even though he was paying for the whole thing, including paying her to help build it. Still, he didn't pay her for all she did. He couldn't have. She was over there so much, different times of day. It was what she was always doing. Meals and sleeping and doing chores at her own house were only interruptions.

She liked having a place to be all the time, the same as when her gramma was still alive.

Her legs were out long and she looked at them in front of her and saw them not the way she always saw herself but the way he would.

He was always daring her to pick him up. He'd say she couldn't; she'd say could too if she wanted. This time, he took his wallet and offered her five dollars if she could lift him just one foot off the ground.

Shelley was known on Keck Road for her strength. When Wesley Janson fell twenty feet down from a telephone pole and broke his arm, Shelley carried him all the way back home, with his bike slung over her shoulder.

The mothers of other girls warned, "Don't you ever get in a fight with her. She looks like a rail, but she's all muscle."

When Shelley locked her arms around George's belly (it was warm; that was kind of a surprise), she didn't know if she really could.

He weighed—what?—probably two hundred pounds.

But she did.

George hired her to do his ma's yard, too, every month or so, when the grass got long. One day, she invited Shelley in for a pop. She had another neighbor there from down the street, the fat woman everyone liked. They were sitting in the dim living room, helping themselves to butter cookies. Shelley felt the slick of her bare legs, with the little flecks of grass on them, smearing the scratchy fabric of the chair.

The fat woman was holding up a photograph in a frame. It was the youngest Umberhum girl, Nell, who was years older than Shelley.

"She was a one that was good in school," George's mother said.

"Oh. Good for her. Isn't that something?"

"She always liked that. She just liked school. Her friends were always glad to get vacation, but she liked school."

That caused a halt in conversation. Shelley had her hand over her mouth. It was good and right to like school; everyone knew it would mean things in that girl's life would probably turn out better than they would in Shelley's, and would also probably take her far far away.

Shelley didn't know really why she didn't like school.

She wasn't dumb or anything, she didn't think. But she was big. And her legs were long and heavy. It was hard to sit at the desk all day and concentrate in the building the bus towed them to every morning, away from their trees and loose air. She got feelings in her toe joints and calves that if she didn't move them, she would die.

She'd had that all her life. Physical limits. Where she just couldn't take it anymore, something had to change.

And now that her own gramma was dead, it seemed odd that this grandmother was still here, in her house, the same.

·   ·   ·

At first, George never let himself go all the way in, even though she wanted him to.

"You gotta be in one piece for your wedding," he said.

In all her life, he was the only one who said the words "wedding" and "you" in the same sentence.

Not even her grandma had supposed she would get married. Her family never spoke about any of that in reference to her.

"'Specially you," he said. "It never bothers me, but some kid doesn't even know you? That's the way it is at that age. They don't know nothing, but they think they do."

"You're strange," she said, socking him in the warm gut.

"I've always been strange," he said. "I've just gotten used to it."

She tried to think, while it was happening, how he saw her leg. Sometimes she imagined it was the part of her he wanted. She pictured her bones the way they might look to somebody else—the dull foot, the slant leg—like a clump of hair growing out where it's not supposed to be, on an elbow, a shin.

When she asked, he told her, "You're different at first, but then you're not. Then you're just young."

It was a small motion like a sawing. She could feel herself hanging on underneath wanting nothing to change, nothing to stop, like that dog, needing the hit hit hit.

Nothing had happened until after her grandma died.

Shelley knew her grandma wouldn't like it. "Other people's lives aren't yours and they aren't going to be," her grandma had said. "You have to think what's interesting for yourself in your own day."

But maybe, Shelley thought, still under him, his shoulder pressing into her collarbone, maybe they are the same. She didn't love him—not la-de-da love, nothing like that. But it was easier after to laugh.

The first time it happened, they were behind the currant bushes, by the cement mixer, bags of the dusty formula stacked around them like a fort. Nance had taken Petey off to get new Keds and then they were stopping at Dairy Queen for Dilly bars.

After that they watched for when she and Petey were gone. They never talked about it. They just noticed and waited. Her grandmother's house was across the way, sitting empty. She still slept there most nights. But they never went inside that first summer. Uncle Bob sometimes walked back and forth in the yard with a stick. It would have required talking about it and planning. They just waited until they were both alone, an acre of hot quiet land ringing around them, and then the air got thicker, making their skin itch and swell.

Only one time, they saw another person: Wesley popping wheelies on his bike in the back of their lawn.

It was never romantic.

They knew each other too much already. Shelley thought it was the opposite of romance, or what she'd seen of that so far. If romance was your heart beating too fast in your chest and your breath shallow and catching, this was more like boredom. Where it was easy to say whatever just walked through your mind.

The only time her body was really like that, when

something felt the way it was supposed to look from the outside, wasn't sex; it was the day they filled the swimming pool. That was already July the second year. They couldn't finish the first summer. They covered up the hole with tarps and bricks when the frost came, and then there was snow damage they'd had to repair. But finally it was done, all the cement poured, the bottom painted—that was what made the color. When they turned the hoses on, the thing just filled, the clear water turning blue when it gained volume.

He let her be the first one. She stood on the diving board for a good long minute, springing on it, feeling the bounce ripple through her legs, up her whole body. Then she threw herself in and felt the surprise.

That was her romance, and she never wore it out. She jumped in every day, liking even the sting in her eyes and her limbs being tossed around in the slam of gravity. She loved swimming in that pool they made. Most of the time, that summer, she was the only one in it.

When Nance and Petey planned a party, she stayed away.

George's being older didn't seem to matter. His being married wasn't what people would have thought, either. That he had all that money built up—those differences seemed eased, blurred away with water.

What could ever happen to end it? she sometimes wondered.

Nothing happened. It never ended, not really, not for thirteen years.

After they finished the pool, the next year they completed the cabana, too. A few weeks later, there was some trouble down at the store and George had to go over and watch them all, make them stop making mistakes.

He said Shelley could come over by the pool anytime she wanted, if he was there or not.

"What'll *she* think?" she said.

"I don't care what she thinks."

Shelley watched from poolside. The sliding glass walls of the kitchen made Nance, with her bright colors and darting motions, look like a fish in an aquarium. When Nance stepped outside, she minced, her high heels clicking on the cement. "Oh George, oh George," she said, in a little squeak, shaking her head at the same time.

The month left of summer after they finished the pool house, Shelley was there most days, sunning her legs on the cement. Nance would be prussing around inside, always in a hurry, not doing much that Shelley could see. Inside, she always wore nylon stockings, with fluffy slippers over them, usually a whole suit above. She looked like she was going to work at a job. But she had no job. She just helped at the store.

"'Cept she isn't any help," George told Shelley.

"Seems like you're mad at her all the time," she said.

"I don't care what she does," he said.

But Nance didn't get much in the way. She talked to the other women on the street about Shelley hanging around the pool all the time, even after the job was done and George back at the store.

"*I thought that was a little funny,*" she'd say.

"*I think so, too,*" would be the answer, no matter which one she talked to.

. . .

But by the middle of September, the leaves were tearing off in the wind. It was too cold by the pool, even in the sun, and Shelley began to think about getting a job.

At first, finishing school had seemed like it always seemed in May, but just a deeper summer, longer. Then it began to dawn slowly, like a train forming out of the air in the distance, that something was over for you.

The main work where she lived was in the canning factories or the paper mills. Shelley put in her applications and waited. She worked first for a year at Schneider Trucking, answering radio calls on the night shift, then for three years she was the secretary at Bay Auto Supply.

All that time, when she was home after work, people saw her around George Umberhum's backyard, at five-thirty, six o'clock. In summer, she'd be by the pool in her swimsuit. In winter, you could see her, tall and a little crooked, small-headed, walking along the perimeter of the yard, in front of the old hedges, picking up sticks and fallen branches.

When George said she could come by the pool anytime, he meant while he was at the store.

He didn't imagine moving or living in another state.

One thing he and Shelley had in common was a love for northeastern Wisconsin. But not Nance.

She wanted to get him to Florida.

And eventually she did.

X

With June, Bea had the endless fugal back-and-forth conversations about love that she had missed as a girl. To anyone else listening, even Hazel, when she had the chance to eavesdrop, these talks sounded repetitive, but they weren't, not exactly. They repeated only the way that scientists review their data when they are stumped, or pianists return to the beginning of a phrase after an error. They reiterated only in order to further refine.

Many nights of 1974 were devoted to the question of whether a woman should telephone a man.

June had a theory about such things. That was one reason Bea liked June; June had a theory about everything.

"See, if a man calls a woman, what does it mean? It means he might be interested or he might just want to see a movie. And if a woman says yes, that means about the same. She doesn't *have* to say yes. Women have been asked out all their lives, so they know how to say no without really saying it. You can always say you're busy or you're so sorry but you just *can't* that night. So if they go out, they're about equal. He's a little interested, maybe, because he asked and she's a little interested because she didn't just say no."

Bea listened, rapt. She had not been asked out all her life, but she was glad June assumed that she had. "But if *she* calls *him* . . . ," Bea said leadingly.

"If she calls him, she seems really interested, not just a little, but really really. Like she's so rabid to see him, she can't wait. And then if he says yes, it doesn't mean what it means when a woman says yes. Because he's not used to being asked. He might just say sure because he doesn't know how to get off the phone. He's maybe so shocked that she called in the first place."

While June explained, Bea knit. At work, Edith's daughter had had a baby, her first baby, premature. This child was getting a soft cashmere blanket, and a snowsuit with tiny shell buttons. She'd opened the box of shipped cashmere yarn that day.

"So let's say they go out. They're on very different footing. She's made it clear that she's interested—boy is she interested—and he's not made anything clear at all. He might not even like her."

"So really she's better off waiting."

"I'd say, waiting and maybe suggesting a little."

Bea brought old things out into the air. The married boss in Chicago who hadn't noticed her.

"If you felt something, he felt something," June said. "You can bet on it."

Bea wondered if that pertained to herself. If Bill Alberts felt something, did she?

"Suggesting like, 'Oh, my dear aunt Betty gave me two tickets to a concert'?"

"Or even, just when you see a poster for a movie, saying, 'Hmm, looks good,' or if he talks about skiing or going to a game, mentioning, 'That sounds like fun.'"

Hazel would've been more than happy to supply her

daughter with this same advice then or any other time during the past twenty years, but Bea would have been mortified to discuss the matter with her parents. Nonetheless, coming from June that night as they paced the kitchen making "quick" tapioca pudding, Bea internalized these rules and remembered them forever.

One of the pleasures of her friendship with Father Matthew was that the rules didn't quite pertain. He wasn't a man in the ordinary sense of the word.

And yet he was. One.

She felt a little racy, phoning Father Matthew at the abbey.

After one such call ("Edith, from my office, gave me some tickets she can't use . . . "), Bea found herself riding with Father Matthew through the West Side, on their way out of town. They were going to a new community theater in what used to be a cornfield. Hazel was supposed to come along, but at the last minute the joints in her fingers hurt.

Driving with Father Matthew was always slow and relaxing. He was so scrupulous, he left lots of time around the edges. He'd arrived early to pick her up and they stayed in the car a full two minutes without actually moving, because someone had once told him that he should idle the engine first, every time, before starting. And in fact, his conscientious obedience had paid off, carwise. He still drove the same Honda, a green one that wasn't even new when they'd met, a full ten years before.

He was the kind of man who ceded his place in traffic. He never asserted himself in conflicts over lanes or parking spaces.

Bea supposed that was what he had in place of the old-fashioned respect her father and a few other men in town still engendered: Father Matthew had the private knowledge that he'd given forth only decency and generosity in the world.

Which was all fine and good, she thought, but it took so damn much time.

Sometimes she just wanted to move a little faster. Their friendship, for example, seemed to be another of his scrupulous projects. She felt quite sure that he never indulged in a moment of petty gossip, that he'd never taken the smallest advantage, never cut into line even when no one but no one was watching. At times, though, she wondered whether this rather general consideration didn't prevent more specific attentions.

It was strange how the West Side had developed. Plains of houses had sprung up in the sixties and seventies, with no main street, no clustered commercial district, no downtown. In fact, the houses seemed to branch right off the new highway itself.

The East Side was Bill Alberts's, but he'd left off here—too busy with the club and with the Fox River Trotters. "What does he need more money for?" Hazel had said. "Already has more money than God."

They passed Van Dam Chevrolet, with its mile-long enclosure of plastic flags, tractors waiting stumped and forlorn, banished to the far edge of the lot.

Bea knew that family, the Van Dams. She'd sold them a lot five or six years ago in a still-wooded development over here, where they built. "Our dream house," they'd called it.

They were rich and felt rich in a way Bea suspected her parents never had, though it was possible, even likely, that their bank balance was equal or superior. When Bea drove her by to see, Hazel had called the Van Dam house an "atrocity." She'd had to take her bun out and pin it back up again. (Bea had made her—per her request—a snood.) But Bea found the odd cathedral refreshing, even exhilarating. The car people's money actually seemed to give them pleasure.

Bea looked over at the driving priest. Despite his uniform jacket—a little in need of dry cleaning or replacement, the fabric "tired," as her mother would've said—this seemed something he, too, would understand.

Large malls opened off the highway. Here, next to a vast Piggly Wiggly, was the big Singer Sewing Center, where you could buy machines, patterns, fabric, and trim. Bea knew that mall well, because the Sewing Center helped her order her yarn. There was one catalog they got for her specially—of nubbly, soft, heavy Italian cashmere blends.

There were restaurants, too, of course, lone restaurants, far apart, each buffeted by a flat tar lot, more parking than you could ever use, and then stray untended field. Everything seemed practical. She saw no charming little place you could duck into for a treat. Ponderosa Steak House. The Sizzler. Big food in big portions. Pound-and-a-half porterhouses. Eight-inch baked potatoes. Nothing delicate or exquisite, nothing small, like at Kaap's downtown, where, in her mother's day, people ate flavored ice creams in colorful molded shapes, and where even now you could get a sundae with the nuts and whipped cream on the side, the hot-fudge sauce in a small pitcher, made of heat-bearing metal, well polished.

Was it possible that the West Side of town was actually western enough to eat more meat?

Father Matthew turned off the highway and drove through some older streets. He stopped the car then at an average corner and said, "There's my folks' place. Where we grew up." He said it just like that.

And there it was. A scrappy yard, with mud paths worn in the lawn, presumably by pets or children. A few bushes, a tree, some rhubarb along one side of the house. Nothing in the yard seemed planned or planted. The house had once been green, but the paint had chipped enough to show the gray boards.

It was a different way of living in a house.

Bea had understood that for the first time not from selling real estate, but from watching June look for an apartment years ago and helping her move in.

In the upstairs flat, June never considered changing a thing except in the most superficial way, with white paint and bamboo shades.

Bea didn't do much to her rental unit, either, but that was just a matter of laziness. She understood that in the realm of the domestic, all was fundamentally malleable. Walls could be moved, shelves put up or taken down, tiles replaced with a different color. (In her life as a real estate agent, Bea had seen people tear out tiles to put in new ones that to her looked indistinguishable from the last.)

June didn't think the owners would allow her to do anything, even if she was willing to spend her own money. She never felt she had permission. She was afraid even to ask.

"But you'd be improving the place," Bea had tried to explain.

"It's theirs, though. What if they didn't like it?"

Bea still remembered June's delight at the few felicitous touches—already there—in the upstairs apartment. That delight had amazed Bea. And all for a deep tub with hot water to last. "It's a seventy-five-gallon heater," Bea explained.

Perhaps Hazel's style—inch by inch, year by year, taking control of every square foot of property and fitting it to her own taste and eye—had deprived her of just that delight at having found something good, beautiful already, without your needing to make it so.

Over the years, Bea had learned that most buyers were like Matthew's parents—one-timers. They bought a house and then got to the business of living in it, more or less as they found it. One of the fascinations of selling houses was seeing how people lived. Sometimes she could even tamper with that.

And there was a beauty to Father Matthew's family house and yard, where nothing seemed ornamental, all strictly for use. His upbringing, no doubt, made it easier to live in the monastery.

As they passed the big Sears, on the highway again, he said, "Remember the Sears catalog? I don't think they have that anymore. Not like they did."

It must have been the trance of these old streets.

"My sisters used to tear into it. They were each allowed to order one new outfit every spring. I think my grandmother paid. And that was the most thumbed-over section of the book. It was that thick then." He held up and opened a hand to show. "One spring, the theme was gingham, red-and-white-checked. Every night, I swear to God."

Bea looked over at him. He didn't take God's name in vain with just anyone.

Bea had never ordered her clothes from a catalog. She remembered her mother taking her to buy her little socks from Em Flato, who wore her eyeglasses on a tortoiseshell chain. She would open an old wooden drawer of anklets in pastel colors, folded like Easter eggs. Bea and her mother would pick. At that time, all the better apparel shops were owned by the Jews in town. Bea once believed these shop owners lived inside their stores, because those were the only places she saw them.

"They'd do the dishes—had to finish your chores first in our house—and then they'd sit at the kitchen table for hours trying to decide what to order. Should it be the white slacks with the red-and-white top? Or the all gingham dress? Or the zip-up jacket, what about that?

"Man. The funny thing is, I'm sure they each finally picked one and ordered it. They must've worn it, probably all that year, but I don't remember ever seeing those checkered outfits on either one of them. I just remember the models in the catalog jumping in jumping jacks. They looked happy. Red-and-white checks. And my sisters, so serious poring over the pages."

Both those sisters were living away now, one in Duluth, one in Milwaukee. He still wrote them letters and called on the phone, especially the youngest, who was going through a rough divorce.

Bea asked how Donna was doing. That sister, once a girl trying to pick the prettiest, most useful gingham, was now a woman of forty, unhappy about the bags under her eyes.

Matthew had saved and was planning to send her the money for cosmetic surgery.

"That seems so un-you," Bea said.

"If it makes her feel better about herself when she looks in the mirror." He shrugged. "People get their peace different ways." He was always a kind, kind man.

Like Bea's own father. But unfortunately for Matthew, he'd entered the priesthood at a time when, in Green Bay at least, his own counsel was less sought. That might have happened to Bea's father, too, if he'd lived a half century later. With all the changes that were coming to medicine.

There were fashions, it seemed, even in veneration.

But Bea's father was lucky. Even now, he was the most trusted pediatrician in town. Bea always assumed that it was because of the general respect for him, so great and taken for granted, that, in the house, he let his wife decide everything. He just did whatever she said.

Theirs was an old friendship.

"It was ten years if it was a day," as Bea heard her mother say recently to Lil, discussing Lil's daughter's divorce.

In the first years, Bea sometimes slid into forgetting that Father Matthew was a priest. It seemed, from the tendencies of their connection, his odd care and intent gestures, that they would tilt into something else, perhaps even something scandalous.

Later, at the time Bill Alberts was pursuing June, it seemed almost certain to Bea that they were heading for a cliff.

During that period, she found her fantasies tangled. It was easy to imagine the *before:* a time and place, the banter as things began to turn and extend just a little bit further than they had. They would stand, hands on hips, and say things to each other until they fell to . . .

To what, exactly, was hard to imagine. But she could easily come up with dialogue.

"But you're a priest!"

"Even priests are men. You are the first woman to . . . "

She had ideas, of course, from magazines and the movies. As she lay in bed in the dark trying to sleep, she couldn't hold the images of models and actresses for long (she could picture them in a pose or a contained movement, but she couldn't make them improvise past what she'd already seen), so she shuffled to parents and her friends. For her, it was difficult to imagine most people in bed, hard to think how they moved, what they felt. The only person she could envision was June. It was easy to picture June unzipping her side-zip pants, moving like a flexible doll into all the positions Bea could think of that a man would want. She saw her friend June's mouth, slack and open, craving.

That was another way Bea used their friendship, all those years, without June ever knowing.

When Bea began to announce her affair to her mother and her father—Father Matthew ceasing to be Father Matthew, giving back his cassocks in a long, flat cardboard box, *but to whom?*—Bea's fantasy tripped her into a state of sit-up alarm.

No, it was impossible to think of an ending together without a degrading scandal. Perhaps that was one reason the culmination had never yet occurred, even in her before-sleep moments of unraveling wishes, taking out her precious jewels on a plate, just to look at. Her fantasies halted. They could kiss but not finish. Her imagination stopped at the place on the neck where a necklace cut.

Now that June was gone, Bea remembered her rules as if they were commandments. She'd broken the ban on calling him—that made no sense; they'd been regular friends for too long—but she'd silently replaced that restriction with the edict that she would never be the one to make a pass.

It had been so long, she was quite sure things would remain more or less how they were. Or, if not forever, at least today. Each time she saw Father Matthew, change seemed less likely. Yet, a few years back, it had seemed impossible that they could endure another talk without touching.

She made a mental note to put Donna on her Christmas list—maybe a muffler.

Though by now, the city and her parents had lived through enough scandals that a little flare-up began to seem as if it might have been worth it.

The protagonists of the local disgraces Bea had watched so far had ended up married and late-middle-aged, concerned with property and money and barbecues, more or less like everybody else.

$\mathcal{B}$ea was offered the listing for June's brother's house in 1975. Nance called her up at the office and said they were moving to Florida. She wasn't sure she wanted to sell; she just wanted to see what kind of money they could get.

"Just sniffing around," Bea said. "All right."

The mother's house, next door, had been sold a few months earlier. Bea looked up the file to see the square footage and the price. June had wanted Bea to list her mother's house, but at that time, Nance and George had given it to someone at another firm, someone Nance played cards with. Which was why the call now was surprising.

Even on the telephone, Bea shied away from the listing, saying (diplomatically, she thought) that it was hard to work on a property you'd known so long yourself.

She'd heard enough from June about Nance. Of course, by then June was gone. She'd moved to Arizona right after her mother died. She used the money she inherited to pay the first and last months on a commercial lease, to open her flower store. Peggy was no doubt already getting used to her new school. But they seemed to Bea somehow diminished, on their own, so far away. Was that because she had most often seen them in her own mother's house, in De Pere?

After all, June had chosen to go.

But Bea regretted now that she hadn't learned more about the financial side of June's life. Likely as not, she could've helped her find a location to open a flower shop here and even gone over the financing.

Bea drove out to June's old road to take a look. It was April but still cold, a hint of ice in the wind. The colors, in the country, seemed full of browns, under the pale blue sky.

Nance met her at the door, holding her lilac cardigan closed at the neck. The minute Bea stepped inside, the woman began following her. She was a person who stood too close behind you. It was an ordinary six-room ranch built in the late forties and now decorated and added on to. Bea had been in the house less than six minutes when Nance asked, "So what do you think we could get?"

Not that Bea couldn't have told her after two.

They were standing in the bright, clean kitchen, walled with sliding glass doors, which gave out to the pool and back-yard compound and didn't do quite enough to insulate from the sharp wind. The stove was dry and still. No tea was offered.

"I've pulled the comparables, from your mother's house," Bea began.

"Mother-in-law," Nance corrected. "And, with the pool and all, this'd be worth a lot more. He's sure put a lot more into it."

Speaking of *he*, Bea was thinking, where was he?

"I can see" was all she said. You couldn't not. Cement surrounded a kidney-shaped pool enclosed by a wooden fence crisscrossed with lights. There was also a two-story pool house, winterized, with a Ping-Pong table set up inside on the first floor.

"I'm in a birthday club," Nance said, "and one of the other girls just bought a house with a pool. And they paid over a hundred thousand dollars for it!"

"On the West Side?" Bea murmured. "I know the property." There weren't that many swimming pools in northeastern Wisconsin. Bea could name each one. The first one in Green Bay was built by the Bishops—wealthy Catholics who had seven kids—during the polio summers of the early 1950s. Bea remembered because some children she knew hadn't been allowed to go to the public pools. Green Bay wealth was not extreme. There was a country club with a pool, yet before and after the polio scare, even girls from Bea's neighborhood went to the public pool in the park, rented lockers, and pinned the keys to their suits. Bea was always allowed to go. Her father believed, as an officer of public health, he had to let his own daughters swim there unless he forbid everyone and went to the city council to see about closing it down. Bea's mother wanted her to stay away and just do other things instead those summers, but as her father's emissary, Bea walked to the public pool and swam. Once, at the height of it, her father rode his bicycle along with her. It was practically a ceremonial occasion—an ordinary July day, and Dr. Maxwell climbed slowly to the top of the high board. When he made a perfect arcing dive, people clapped. For a while, children were supposed to shower before stepping into the pool. After that, they had to stand in a second shower, where they were sprayed with a blue disinfectant. People told their children not to drink from bubblers. "Don't kiss boys or you might end up with a crooked leg," Hazel said. That was at the same time the county passed an ordinance to pick up all stray cats and put them to sleep. Bea and her father were against this measure, too, and they drove out together at night, slowing the car and looking for stray cats to adopt before the animal catchers found them.

The pool Nance was talking about was new, in a wooded development opened up seven or eight years ago, when the highway was widened. The house was architect-designed, redwood.

"So I was thinking," Nance said, "we may as well ask something like that. Maybe even a little more, cause they're getting more land here?"

All Bea wanted was to leave politely. She intended to behave decently to June's brother's wife, as a matter of honor; at the same time, also as a matter of honor, she didn't want to collude with her in any way.

"Maybe a hundred ten?" Nance whispered.

Where *was* he?

This house was a case of serious overdevelopment.

One of the hallmarks of Bea's practice had always been fair pricing, and she often spent quite a bit of time with owners before she agreed to list a house. For Bea, most of the work came before. She hired a niece of Beth Penk's to do a thorough cleaning for her open houses; this woman knew to stack things so they looked nice, even if the owners didn't. Bea herself went through and rearranged, tied together bundles of *National Geographics* and piled them in the garage. In almost every case, she made the houses barer. One of her clients had coined the term *Maxwellize,* from the dry cleaner's "One-Hour Martinizing." Two times, couples changed their minds about selling after Bea's ministrations. And her sellers almost always resented the new owners, feeling they would get something out of the house that they themselves had, in their years of possession, missed.

By the end of the day of an open house, Bea usually had her sale. She presented the new owner with a dark brown "new home throw," something several sellers told her they acutely coveted. But I can't start doing both, Bea told herself.

They'd built quite a compound here. Back behind all the carnival effects of the pool, with its clown colors and uneven cement, Bea could see the hedge of currant bushes and, beyond that, the field and then the highway, looping around to the overpass going to Sheboygan.

"George says we can get a hundred thousand," Nance said.

A hundred thousand, my foot, Bea thought. She doubted George even knew about this meeting.

"I'm not the right agent for you." She had to say it. "We tend to stay very close to the comparables. That's too conservative an approach for some sellers. You may want a more aggressive agent."

Nance gave her a look. More aggressive than *you*? it seemed to say. You with your job like a man who did Lord knows what in Chicago.

"Well, how does it work?" Nance finally said. "Don't we tell you the price?"

Bea looked down.

"Because I don't know why we wouldn't get what the other one with the pool got."

Asked so directly, Bea murmured something about the location, being farther away from things downtown. That house being newer, too.

"Why don't you just put it up and try? What work is it for you? You've already got the signs and all."

"I won't list at a price I'm not confident of getting. Now, believe me"—Bea jittered into an imitation of laughter—"I've often been wrong." Not true, not true, bells were ringing.

Nance didn't like her. Bea could see it around her mouth. Fair enough.

A good many people disliked her and Bea knew it. They considered her dangerous. A gossip. A snoop. All because she was thirty-eight years old and remembered a thing or two.

At the door, before leaving, Bea couldn't resist. "What do you hear these days from June?"

"Oh, you know June," Nance said. "Same as ever. Peggy's real good, though. Doing all honors in school."

June could be exasperating; no one knew that more than Bea. But she was the best friend Bea had ever had. In the months she'd been gone, Bea had done a great deal of thinking. She remembered, in particular, how her mother had talked June out of Bill Alberts.

It was true enough; June hadn't loved him. Not in the way they'd wanted love and still hoped for it. But that day when she'd imitated him, she'd been flimsy. They probably could have convinced her in his favor, too. And how different her life now would be, and Peggy's.

Still, June wrote with their news, accepting Arizona as their life, as if there had been no possible other.

June had asked them, trusting. And Bea and her mother had decided it for her. Yet June might have loved living here, along the river, gathering red and brown leaves for centerpieces at the Harvest Moon Ball, as Mrs. Bill Alberts.

Bea had always had her parents' house.

June called, once a month or so, always on weekends, when the rates were down, to hear the gossip. Even though

Bea and her mother had perhaps taken something from them, something large, June showed no blame.

Bea knew her own reasons, obliquely. She needed Bill Alberts where he was—for a little longer. But what was her mother's motive? Certainly her mother wasn't thinking about love—not that kind of love, not then, at this time in her life.

Could June have come to love him, later, in a different way? That was an old model of marriage, not much in favor now, based on an exchange of work and gifts, a system of gratitude, but one that would probably go as well as any other, from what Bea observed.

"Well," Bea said. "I guess she's having a success with her store."

"Oh, that she can do," Nance said.

Bea clutched the wheel, driving too fast down the small road. She had it in mind to call June, or type her a little note. June would get a kick out of the circus lights, the hurried tour, the whispers, George nowhere to be seen.

This listing, Bea was glad to forgo.

There were no mysteries in pricing, to her mind. None. A little room for romance on the edges: a good wooden floor, a mature garden. Trees. Bea sometimes took over a bread pan and a loaf of the bread Hazel bought frozen but not yet baked, but really, no smell could ever spirit away Highway 141 or the house near the end of Keck Road with broken dolls and car-body parts rusting on the front lawn.

That day, turning onto the highway, she passed an unusually handsome boy, who must have been thirteen or fourteen, with his arm flung around a girl, their bodies tall and so perfect, they actually looked plain—as if the ordinary human model should be *this*.

I should have told them to wait, she thought. Pools don't show well in winter. The trick to selling that house would be to ring those handsome country kids around that pool. Then she wondered if the pool had ever really been used. Maybe they'd had parties—barbecued on the cement, passed out leis and hot dogs, roasted marshmallows, but it was hard to picture. From what she remembered, they'd built that pool just a few years back.

Bea's judgment proved right.

She followed the property. The house wasn't listed at all until 1979, and then they had it with someone at Knoll, Handower. It was for sale over a year before they came down on the price. In the end, they sold to an assistant manager at Shopko for $43,000, less than half of what they were first asking, only four thousand more than the old mother's house next door.

And June really had gone away and stayed gone.

All the years she'd talked with June those nights in her mother's kitchen, the thing they'd wanted, the thing endlessly analyzed, the thing they both held up as the prize, was love. Of the married-and-living-together-in-a-house-in-Green-Bay variety.

They were both keenly sensitive to shams and spent more of their hours picking apart the marriages they knew and wouldn't want than enunciating the secrets of the ideal they both still pretended to believe in.

When June left for Arizona, she was thirty-seven.

After a while, Bea wondered if that kind of love still was the real prize or if it had been like the committees she'd joined in high school and clubs in college—a subject to trade wits on, to organize daily talks, to help her make a friend. Even later, it occurred to her that it might still be that, for others, too, not only for herself. June, in their conversations from Arizona, also sounded distinctly less inclined toward romance.

Of course, Peggy was growing up. Peggy's upbringing—achieved on her own, supported now by the flower store—that was most of June's life.

Getting out of teaching and opening a flower shop—those had always seemed June's driving goals. But now that she had one, the shop became a duty and an agitation, like any job. It struck Bea that June's real concern all along must have been her daughter. Maybe flowers were merely her best means of supporting her child. And from what Bea heard, that had worked. Her business was booming, and in college, Peggy was able to afford many of the normal things a girl would want, things June couldn't have provided on a teacher's salary. "I'd hoped to do it in high school," June said over the phone, "when she'd still be here, so I could see her in the clothes."

What had Bea been thinking all those years, with her grand romance about flowers?

No, sending Peggy off to college was an achievement for June, as much or more than any love they'd talked about. Why was that the only thing, marriage? Bea had friends, work, hobbies, golf, loads of laughter. Bea looked back at those promising conversations they'd had with a certain bitterness. They'd assumed such *futures*.

. . .

By now, Bea's mother was truly baffled. How was it that someone like Bea got left out? Could it be true that a life offered just so many chances, and that was it? Even if so, when were those, her daughter's?

Could Hazel have missed them somehow?

Lil's old joke rang tauntingly in her ear. Lil, who'd taught piano all her life, told her pupils about the tuner named Operknockety, who refused to come back after he'd tuned an instrument. *Operknockety tunes only once.*

Maybe it had all happened, chance and refusal, in Madison or Chicago. Chicago, probably. So that now it truly was over, all the questions answered with the small word *no*, without her mother having ever had even the momentary swing of hope between interrogation and its conclusion.

Hazel took out a pin from her hair and scratched her now-furrowed brow. With a walker, her sight murky and unreliable, she darted too close to her daughter—sometimes she couldn't help herself from blaming Bea—and fiercely tore open a button or two of Bea's blouse. "Show a little," she rasped. "With that buttoned all the way up to the top, you look like some little schoolmarm."

But you saw fat people, ugly people, lame people, for heaven's sake, all kinds of people with one deficit or another, who went on in life, married, had children. Plenty divorced and then did it all over again.

But what about her Bea? She looked at her daughter's virginity, housed in a large, handsome, middle-aged woman, and it made her shudder.

At a card game long ago, she'd sat with her three best friends around a felt-covered square table—spades, hearts, clubs, and diamonds appliquéd in brown felt over the red. They'd talked about their teenage daughters' virginities. Lil was pretty sure both her girls had been deflowered by the same boy. She spoke ruefully; Hazel truly pitied her, and at the same time, she was shocked. He was a blond boy from a nearby dairy farm who'd been working at the club for the summer. Yes, she was pretty sure, she said. Caz had only boys, and Jen said she didn't know, although the others at the table thought they did. Jen's girl was established around the dance hall at Bay Beach, from what they'd all heard. That night, Hazel felt more than sorry for Jen and Lil. She'd felt embarrassed by her own child's lack of problems.

"Oh, I don't know," she'd finally said about Bea. "I think she's still in the dark, but what do I know."

The others had rushed in to reassure her about her daughter's virtue, about which she'd truly had no doubt. And Bea's virginity, that night, had seemed an erectness in her posture, something symmetrical, silver.

XII

When Shelley turned twenty-five, she got the house. Ten years earlier, after her gramma died, they told her the house and the retirement bonds had been left to her. She offered the house to Uncle Bob, to let him live there, but he said no, he'd just as soon stay where he was, up top the garage. She found out she was old enough now to have the house in her own name when she received a bill for the property tax in the mail. "That I'll gladly pay," she said.

But Shelley's mom and dad distributed things. That was how it went in their family. Sharing was less an ideal than a necessity. Nobody owned anything personally, not if another one had a good reason to need it. Sometimes their mother took pride in how many uses she could wring out of a particular item, amortizing the expense. There was a vest she'd once bought for Boo Boo. Tim had it for his prom, it worked as part of Shelley's costume for a school play (she was cast as a guard), Dean wore it when he flew over to his sister's wedding, and now the vest waited in Germany for Kim's youngest to grow into it.

Only Dean got to go to the wedding. He was single and working at Fort Howard, so he had the bucks. But they all set their alarms to watch when Princess Diana of England had her wedding. They wanted it to be like that for Kimmie over in Germany.

Her brother Butch—still called Boo Boo—joined the army. He came home in his uniform right before he shipped out to Fort Ord, but when Shelley remembered him, she saw him in his first uniform, for Scouts, with that first gun, his teeth even and small and his face so round like a pumpkin.

With the little bank money from her grandmother, Tim was still going to school. He just kept on; he was already way past college. He still worked for the nursery, and they were helping him out, too. Kimmie had needed money for her wedding, so Shelley had signed the papers to liquidate the bonds. Kim got a third and Tim almost a third and Butch and Dean each a little less and then she was done with it. Shelley still had the house. She'd been living there now almost a decade. She moved in while she was still in high school.

She lived in it just the way it was. She never really thought of it as her house. It was her grandma's still. That was what she liked about it. After so long, the smells stayed in the closets. Shelley would open the medicine cabinet where her gram had kept the Mentholatum and the Band-Aids and the camphor and hand towels, and for a while, she could forget time. When she opened a wardrobe, cylinders of denser air turned, faintly dancing in her grandmother's coats.

She often fell asleep in the easy chair in front of the bluey TV, where her gram had sat. She still had electricity and gas and cable, but her mom and dad had canceled the phone. She used it so little, it was a waste of money; they figured she could always walk across the yard to theirs, but she almost never did. In those days, she was a person one other person had loved once. That was her dose, and she was prepared to settle for it and take what warmth was left in the house. Once, that was all.

She had tried working. When they told her at Bay Auto Supply that they were phasing out her job, what with the new computer system, she decided to go back to school. She picked Vocational Nursing because she'd always liked taking care of her gram. And she could study that right downtown.

For her first job, she got sent to Bill Alberts.

She had never met anybody like him before.

She wasn't sure if she'd like being a nurse.

"What did I know?" she said later. "Classes, you can't tell."

She had never been able to listen in school. She often lost the beginning of what the teacher was saying, and then it was an agony watching the clock, hoping the teacher wouldn't call on her. She could be lucky for a few days, but then it would come again, the humiliation of not knowing the answer. She never guessed or goofed. She said "I don't know" right away, looking down seriously.

The vocational classes were held at night in the old brick YMCA building. There was lots about nutrition, babies, neonatal patients, people with lifelong pain. Shelley was not so interested in babies. She'd had enough of babies at home. They even talked about wardrobe, what to wear for the interview. You were supposed to have two jackets, three skirts, four blouses, and so forth. And for hairstyle, they said to go to an experienced beautician and get a flattering cut. Then you could have someone in your family take pictures of your head from all different angles so a cheaper barber or even someone you knew could copy the shape.

The teachers understood that everyone had already worked all day. People wore factory uniforms. One guy from the paper mill stunk of chemicals that burned Shelley's eyes, but still she didn't change seats. And the students were different ages. None of them knew one another, so nobody was popular and nobody was not.

When the woman in the job-placement office asked, Shelley just wrinkled her face. "Don't like babies," she said. And the woman was right in her hunch. Shelley was good with old people. From being with her gramma, probably. Big oinking noises from the bathroom didn't frighten or disgust her. She stayed where she was, outside the door, waiting to be called.

The first day, when she met Bill Alberts, she said, "Jeez, is this all one house?"

Shelley had seen the place before. It was one of the mansions on Mason, the one made of river stones that Mr. Kaap had built with his money from the restaurant and bakery. Kaap had still been alive, in his restaurant, when Shelley was small. With five kids, her family didn't go out to eat much, just Christmas; and she remembered, one Easter, going to pick up a pink box of cookies her mom had selected, pointing to them behind the case, one by one by one.

She'd been to a doctor's office on the bottom floor of one of these old mansions. The doctor had treated her for free, put hot packs on her legs and given her stretching exercises. Then they walked to the candy store, and each time, he'd given her pennies to pick her own gum balls, different colors. "One for each day till you come again," he said, "so you won't get polio in the face." But when she got home, of course, she had to share the loot with her brothers and sister. One time, two dressed-up ladies took her out to Kaap's for ice cream.

She'd got a lot of attention for the polio the first few months, but then the spoiling petered out. She didn't have it bad, and everyone probably figured she'd recovered. As much as she was going to anyway.

She thought most of these old mansions by now were apartments or offices. A couple realtors had a floor in another one, the company that sold Gram Umberhum's place when she died.

"All one house," he said. "But I don't climb steps anymore. Not with this hip." He pointed with his cane. "So the second and third floor can be your playroom."

"You're planning for me to live here?"

"Sleep here nights, Sunday through Friday, that's what they told me. During the day I'm in the office with a lot of people. Nights are when I need someone, strictly speaking. And it's a just-in-case kind of situation. Most nights, you can just sleep. Is that a problem for you? Say now or forever hold your peace."

"They told me nights. I just didn't know you wanted me to live here, live like *live*, bring-my-stuff kind of live."

"Oh, I don't know, either. This is the first time I've had a nurse. You'll have to pardon me. I'm new at this."

She grinned. "I'm new, too. Just finished up over at Central."

"Well, we can make it all up ourselves, then." He tapped the lens of his glasses with a finger. "I've never been much of a chef, so I take most of my meals out. Have you eaten lunch?"

That was how they started. Eating out at a restaurant.

This ain't too bad, she was thinking. I can stand this.

"Shelley," he said to her that first day. "Like Shelly Manne. You share a name with one of the great jazz drummers, who, moreover, is in my personal Great Jewish Jazz Drummers Hall of Fame."

"Huh?" Shelley said. The Packers had a Hall of Fame here in town, but she'd never been to it.

"See, I'm a drummer. One of a long line."

"You got a drum set?" she asked.

"Yes ma'am."

They went to all kinds of restaurants. He would read about a restaurant in the newspaper and want to try it.

Shelley thought they made a gooney pair. He was five foot three and bald as an egg, with black glasses. Shelley stood six one, even stooping.

Of course, she didn't have the sort of clothes the other people in those restaurants wore. She never did build up her wardrobe from following the markdown sales, the way the lady had suggested in night school. She just went in her regular shorts and T-shirts, figuring she was working. This perturbed her mother no end, her mother, who was fascinated by the idea of Shelley eating in places like that. She called Kimmie in Germany to tell her, but Kimmie seemed less riveted by her sister's meals. She was far away, in a military-housing two-bedroom, with babies who woke up at night crying for bottles every three hours.

After Shelley worked for Bill Alberts a month, she couldn't believe all the things she hadn't known about before. She got so she could tell the difference between different salads. Salad! Before, she didn't even eat salad, she told him. He made fun of her because she liked to go to Kroll's on her nights off and get a chili burger and press the soft bun flat between her fingers. She still liked regular food, the food she used to eat, sandwiches, she also pressed flat. Sometimes she would miss a liverwurst sandwich and then just make one. Now she cut off her own crusts.

She started to cook in his kitchen. She noticed the things he liked. Some you couldn't get in stores, so she had her mother plant them in her garden, a certain kind of green bean called *haricot vert*.

She drove his old Cadillac to Madison because there was a horn player he wanted to hear. He knew a restaurant where they made a special kind of meat with cherries in the sauce, and he was remembering that.

After dinner, they went to a club where Ruby Braff played with local pickups. "The Armstrong style," he said, and listened for hours and hours. She didn't ask anything, but thought, Armstrong, Armstrong. It made her think of a man with muscles she'd seen on TV commercials, something to do with kitchen floors. But maybe that was Mr. Clean. Shelley sat in the corner reading a magazine. When the little candle on her table guttered out and she couldn't see anymore, she dug a clipper from her pack and went at her nails, feeling the hard edges in the dark.

XIII

One day, during Bea's years of watching her mother, Dr. Maxwell up and died. Bea and her mother were stunned, though no one else was.

"Here we were always worrying about *her*!" Bea told people at work, her voice incredulous.

In the office, after he closed the door, Bill Alberts said to Edith, "'Her' will live to be a hundred. Hazel's an ox. A miniature ox."

Dr. Maxwell died the way he'd done everything else in his life—quietly, without fuss, essentially alone. The evening before, wearing his tweed hat, he'd driven his wife to Kaap's for dinner.

Apparently, he'd complained that night of indigestion and had taken two tablets of Alka-Seltzer before bed. (Two tablets—an advertising decision Bea remembered reading about. Some clever copywriter thought, Why not say two and double sales?)

Hazel hadn't thought anything of the indigestion, because he'd ordered the creamed shrimp on toast, and Kaap's had already gone down quite a bit by then. Once, Father Matthew and Bea saw a cockroach scaling the wall of their booth.

After the doctor died, Bea and her mother cleared out his office. Hazel would have hired some college girl to do it, but Bea insisted that they sift through the items one by one. Behind the closet door hung an old poster of Elvis with his sleeve rolled up, getting inoculated. The files of living patients and most of the instruments could be simply passed on to the younger pediatrician he'd worked with—one of Lil's twins, now divorced, the girl who used to eat half a head of lettuce for supper.

Most files of the dead were already in the hospital basement. There was a locked cabinet marked EXTREMELY CONFIDENTIAL. DO NOT OPEN. Only one key existed, and it now belonged to her mother. Without exactly acknowledging what they were doing, they saved that cabinet for last.

Dr. Maxwell's collections had to be dispersed. He had nests, including a hummingbird's, the size of Bea's thumb; abandoned eggs and bones of all kinds, bee skeps and a wasp's dome that looked like petrified cotton candy. He'd kept these things around his office for the children to look at while they waited for their appointments. Bea packed them each up. Her mother didn't want any of it in the house.

"Too much dirt," she said. "That's why he kept it all here. I wouldn't let him bring it home in the first place. Those nests are full of bugs."

But Dr. Maxwell had never worried about bugs or dirt. He always said, "Let them eat dirt. It builds immunity."

It was rainy the day Bea carried her father's treasures from her car into the Brown County Museum, so she covered the box with dry-cleaning plastic. Marion Betz locked up once she'd let Bea in, then led her to the back stockroom, where they stood together unpacking and labeling Dr. Maxwell's collection. Dr. Maxwell had been the pediatrician for Marion's three children, who were now all grown, living other places. The room was dim, with high windows, the rainfall exaggerated by the metal roof, and Marion made a delicious tea that tasted of cinnamon, heating the water in a tin pan on an electric hot plate. Strange boxes filled the metal shelves, random odd materials, even rolls of what looked like insulation.

From what Bea gathered, Marion cleaned and maintained the exhibits and led tours for schoolchildren.

When Bea left, she was leaving, too, Marion said. That was why she'd locked up early. She was going to drive out to the old prison camp. In the 1960s, men in the penitentiary had been rewarded for good behavior by being let out to work in the woods. They'd cultivated a portion of the forest, building paths, putting in metal rides, swings, barrels, and a merry-go-round.

For a long time, that area had been a vague public park called the Reforestation Camp. Bea and June had often hiked there on Sundays. Bea had a picture from one picnic with Bill Alberts—at the time he was courting June, or her, or was it both of them?—wearing a corduroy jacket with patches, and a bow tie.

Now that place was the site of the new zoo. It no longer seemed so far out of town, either, and it had lost its quaint, slightly sinister feel. It was one of the main family tourist attractions of Green Bay. There was a glossy pamphlet about it offered at the information kiosk near the car rentals in the airport. But people had once been afraid to take their children there.

"They're the *good* prisoners," June used to say when another mother questioned her, the mother of a friend Peggy wanted to bring along.

What did they expect? Chain gangs? Abductions?

The prisoners did the maintenance. They kept the trails clear and cleaned the cages of the few animals. Bea recalled a skunk, a raccoon, maybe even a badger, the state mascot. All local beasts, not the colorful exotics of today, most of which would never normally be found in North America. And Bea didn't remember ever hearing that anything had happened to a child there. Nothing done by any of those men.

Now Marion Betz was driving out in her Taurus wagon to the old camp office with her camera and tape recorder. She was writing up the history of the place. She would also gather the Popsicle-stick models the prisoners had made, and the animal keepers' chronicles of daily feedings, animal illness, birth and death.

It would make a good exhibit. And the ground trails families still walked on, the tall trees they hushed under, would be remembered for their planters and keepers—for a little while longer at least.

Running out to her car, the box, now empty, held over her head to keep it dry, Bea thought that jobs, many of them—hers, Marion's—could grow or contract. You could push the edges out more and more or you could do so little that you barely did anything at all.

After June left, Bea spent a good six years on the Vander-mill development, starting with the paperwork and bank loans, all the way through to sod and planted trees. Since then, she'd been casting about, selling the odd house here or there, waiting for another big project. Last summer, she'd even driven down to Shell Lake for a knitting camp, never again.

Since her father died, Bea had reached an all-time point

of diminishment. Soon she would have to rev up a little. At the very least, she'd have to list her father's office.

When Bea and her mother finally opened the cabinet of confidential files, they found old secrets, mostly irrelevant now. Which pregnancy was a well-liked teacher's fault and how and where it ended, whose knife wound was given by everyone's favorite mother. Most of the parties by now were dead or moved. Apparently, secrets expired, too. Whether passed among people, used, or kept lifelessly in a dim jar.

"Like Christmas cake," her mother mumbled, "worth nothing the day after."

Bea had heard that said about a girl's virginity.

Her mother had certainly taken plenty of care over that. She'd kept her daughter inside, a secret. But then she'd missed the date she should've set her out with a flourish, as the centerpiece. That's what the South knew how to do, with its debutante balls.

Maybe her mother was only waiting for her to blossom, be ready to wear the weight of all those eyes. There were pictures of her sister, Elaine, all through the house. Elaine as a baby, Elaine in a swing, Elaine set atop a pony. Elaine went through a bad stage, then turned beautiful and stayed there. Even now, though she'd thickened with motherhood. Hazel kept waiting for Bea to turn. There were very few pictures of Bea.

Also, Hazel knew too much. As the wife of Dr. Maxwell, she knew what happened to girls, even to the best girls, from the old families. She never once told a friend, although several times over the years, their speculation, their gossip, came close to a mystery she understood. Then she had no choice but to become very quiet, as she had been when her husband talked, lying next to her in the dark bed at night.

The doctor's confidentiality stopped with her; she was where he placed his secrets. Yes, she had been a good doctor's wife.

But what about her details, her secrets?

Now, sometimes, she wondered if she should have been less scrupulous. Her friends might've talked to her more about Bea. No, she had kept silent and held her daughter's secrets aloft, when she would've been better off as one of the crowd. She'd never laid her real problems out on the table. That would have seemed to her a betrayal of Bea. But would it have been?

Marie Winslow, the most beautiful girl in twenty years, had been made pregnant by an older man in town, a married person who was still alive. Still married.

Girls were brought in from the country for virginity checks.

Even repairs.

One mother demanded stitches. "Doctor, it was a—I don't want to say the word, but it wasn't her fault. The equivalent of a theft."

"And who was the thief?"

"Someone we thought was a friend. Who was staying with us."

A young man who was now thriving down in Milwaukee—a city councilman—had grown up his whole life a hermaphrodite.

That baby of Marie's—it was a big child, too, coming out of that slim underage girl. Marie returned afterward, but she was never the same. Hazel always imagined the delicate beautiful shelf of a hipbone, cracked.

Bea watched her mother finger through the files, trembling. Her father had been a modest man, too fearful. "I'm no Jonas Salk," he used to say.

These had been her secrets, too, which she had kept for her husband. Perhaps at some expense to herself.

And now what were they? Old files. Yellowed, flaking.

What had she expected to find here? Something about herself?

Laid horizontally on top of the neat wedged files was a clipping from *The Press Gazette*. Also brittle, frail, headlined GREEN BAY'S ONLY CASE OF POLIO. DOCTORS BELIEVE IT CAME FROM THE VACCINE. In the photo, Shelley sat posed between her parents. They all three seemed to be wearing their best clothes, smiling.

XIV

ill Alberts took Shelley to the car lot and asked what color she liked.

"Your car, you decide; doesn't matter what I like."

He looked at her a strange way, his gaze flat, like a knife. "You don't think I could drive, at my age?"

"I'll drive whatever color you want. Still your car."

"Now, what am I going to do with a car I can't drive?" He sighed. "You lose interest. In so many things."

Shelley thought restaurants were the real reason he bought her the Jeep Cherokee wagon. He probably wanted to go back to Madison and get some more of that meat with the cherries in the sauce. She made up her mind to duplicate that sauce. Usually, if she tasted something twice, she could do it at home. If they were someplace and he loved a dish with a flavor she couldn't identify, she'd say she had to go to the bathroom and walk right into the kitchen and ask the cook. Most times, the cook told her.

She picked red.

He spent an hour haggling with the salesman, arranging for the car to be delivered to a store on the outskirts of town where a certain sound system he had in mind could be installed. He wanted the speakers to be just so. Jazz was the one thing that still interested him.

Every night, after dinner in a restaurant, she took him to the Riverclub and got him settled at his table. That was their routine. He had a drum set there and another at home. Most nights, he didn't play anymore, but he always listened. And he talked to his friends. Shelley never stayed. The whole Port Plaza mall was now open late, and she would take a drink from the bar and wander through the lighted indoor streets, stores winking on both sides.

He put the red truck in Shelley's name.

"What if I quit you?" she asked.

"I'll be out a truck and a girl," he said.

That was the first time she really thought, I lucked out.

More times followed. And during the first year, no one seemed to notice that he was buying her things. The Jeep was first, but that probably seemed to most people a necessary perk of the job. Those who knew it was in Shelley's name thought there must be some good reason, likely having to do with insurance, and that if Shelley left, the car would decently revert to the next nurse.

"You probably don't remember it here before the mall," Bill said. They were downtown in December. The Jeep was already almost two years old.

"Oh, yeah, I was born yesterday, sure."

This was one of their themes, a tree many small jokes grew out of. All the things Shelley didn't remember because she wasn't even alive then.

Bill Alberts thought it was somehow terribly funny that

there was a Shelley at all. Someone born so long after every-thing he cherished had already ended. Someone younger than his own children, who were all in the East, two in med-ical schools, like his parents. Having children had worked out well, he thought. Could've had even more. The youngest, about whom he'd worried least, were turning out just as well, maybe better. Could have had six.

But Shelley did too remember the old Main Street, when only Kendalls was six stories and all the other stores were low.

Keck Road was just far enough out that her family had made coming downtown their Christmas trip. They drove in to eat an early supper at Kaap's, in one of the dark wooden booths with little hexagonal lights: hamburgers on rye bread, the meat bleeding through and mixing with the odd, sweet, hot mustard. Over the bar, a lighted picture of a waterfall seemed to perpet-ually renew itself, making rushes, jumping foamy waves—provided by a Wisconsin beer company. Their mom and dad ordered Tom and Jerrys and let the kids sip the fluff. Their dad drank in gulps, so they could see his Adam's apple bobbing, while their mom took an eternity, eating it with a spoon.

On the way out, they passed through the wide hallway of dark wood, murals, and more dim tiny lights, and then, in the foyer, the bakery case on one side, full of colored cookies in the shapes of fruits, on the other side all the fancy candies, little bars, cased in paper, the foil ends glittering, with beauti-ful painted scenery from Switzerland.

Their mom and dad always used to joke about the cash register. Mr. Kaap's ancient, bone-thin sister Mabel worked there. She lurched over the keys as if her tiny fingers were attached with strings. People said she was there every night of the year, Thanksgiving too and Christmas. When she got old, they stopped the joking.

Everyone knew she died there, standing. There were no children anywhere in the family. All the property was sold and left to Bea Maxwell, to distribute to charity. Mabel Kaap hadn't known Bea well. She just remembered her collecting for March of Dimes.

After Kaap's, Shelley's parents took the children to see the windows at Kendalls. There were other stores on North Main, brick buildings, each a little different, but all she remembered were the mechanical windows of Kendalls, each perfect like a page inside a book.

Now that she understood what Jewish was, it seemed odd that the Kendalls had gone to all that work making the windows with their lights.

"Business," Bill Alberts said, shrugging. "To them it was business."

Shelley and her brothers and sister rode around town in their father's cement truck, starting with the big neighborhoods. It was a real show. People went to trouble, whole scenes blinking on and off in their front yards. The wide, many-windowed mansions had mostly Santas and reindeer. They wound through the streets and blocks slowly, farther and farther out—where, in the small houses with only one front window, they saw more crèches—until they ended up near where they started, at their own church, Saint Philip's, for the midnight Mass.

And now Shelley was on the top floor of Kendalls and he was telling her to try on this and this and this, getting ready to buy her more.

Shelley knew she'd cheated. She hadn't even gone to a four-year school. What was she doing in these same dressing rooms with the doctors' wives and the career women?

"I don't need such stuff," she said as he was piling things

onto the wooden register desk. "I'm fine with what I've got." Shelley stood with her hands in her pockets, as if chastened, the way athletes sometimes look dressed up in regular clothes.

Just then, Bea Maxwell appeared from behind a mirror, where she was looking at herself holding a big leather sack made to look like the ones mailmen carried. Her leg canted out a certain way, her heel lifted from her shoe.

"Spiffing up the girl," she whispered to Bill Alberts after hellos were said all around and Shelley ducked her head down behind the racks. "Christmas bonus," he said.

"A bonus for you, too." She laughed.

Bea said she'd been on the first floor buying ribbon for her Christmas balls. On Christmas Day, Bea and her mother gave a formal sit-down lunch for nineteen, and Bea presented every guest with a ball made of cloves stuck into an orange. Bea was known for these clove balls, and people would ask her how far along she was. In Kendalls, she told Bill Alberts, "Half-done. Ten more to go. It *is* the seventeenth of December." Several people in the office had offered to buy them, so of course she felt obliged to give each of them one, though without inviting them to the lunch.

If you were a woman in Green Bay, eventually you took up something you did for Christmas. Marion Betz at the museum gave old pots she found in junk stores, planted with forced bulbs. The only man Bea knew who entered into this ritual of exertion was Father Matthew, who was famous in a small circle for leaving a glass milk bottle filled with his own homemade eggnog (spiked) outside your door in the snow. He didn't even write notes or cards; you just knew it was from him. Bill Alberts made a trip to the bank to get unfolded bills for his cash bonuses. The older Bea became, the less it seemed to her that most men participated in festivities at all. They attended.

Shelley was hunched by the cash register, stubbornly repeating that she didn't want any of it.

"Ta-ta," Bea said, excusing herself.

Watching her walk away, a tall woman in expensive woolen clothes, Shelley suddenly missed her own family.

On the wooden escalator going down, while Bill Alberts was trying to convince her that no one deserved such things, that every woman who shopped on that floor had luck every bit as random as hers—Bea Maxwell, for example, who was just born rich—Shelley got the idea that she'd like to buy her mother one of those coffee machines. They probably had them here in the gourmet basement.

Bill's old nanny had taught Shelley how to make his coffee in the morning and she'd gotten to like it, too. It was the one thing about his life she thought she probably couldn't give up and go back to the old way. Later on, it turned out, there was quite a bit more. One of the restaurants Bill Alberts went to took his favorite dish off the menu—noodles made with tomatoes and wild mushrooms. She'd said, "I can try and make that." She didn't measure or look at books. And by now, she'd transformed Mabel Kaap's German rose beds into a kitchen garden, with corn, tomatoes, peas. She'd shrugged when Bea Maxwell mentioned the roses. "He likes food. Different kinds of stuff."

The one time Shelley's mom had come to visit at his house

while he was out at work, Shelley had made a pot of his coffee and even she liked it.

Downstairs, Shelley picked out the whole works—the machine, the grinder, filters, beans, everything—and paid with her own money, cash. He stood there next to her and didn't offer, but she was wondering the whole time if he would. She wouldn't have let him, no way.

By the time they got to the Jeep she wasn't mad at him anymore. Here he was paying her to help him and he was carrying two big shopping bags of new clothes for her.

He looked at her in a funny way. Maybe because of the polio, he thought she needed fixing up. "A fixer-upper" was what she'd heard Bea Maxwell say to him about a house they were selling.

The one thing he really wanted to give her was music. In the house and in the car, he played her his favorites: Chet Baker, Bill Evans, Charlie Parker. She couldn't really follow it. "It's your dime," she always said when he asked if she minded.

She didn't mind when he had it on, but it shook right off of her. Most of it sounded the same to her. She couldn't tell one from the other, any more than she could with rain, a different day's rain. She preferred songs with words, ones about love.

That night, she wanted to drive out to her ma's. She called Bea Maxwell to see if she could take him home from the Riverclub.

Big surprise. Bea said she'd be glad to.

Shelley liked driving out to Keck Road in the Jeep. She used to go weekends to her gramma's house, but not every weekend, since George and them moved to Florida. So last summer, when her mom asked could Dean and Cathy stay there just to get on their feet again after the baby, she'd had to say yes.

The house wasn't really her gramma's anymore. The smells would all be different now, what with baby stuff. Shelley didn't even like to go in.

She parked in the drive behind her dad's truck and went through the kitchen door. They had never used the front door as a door. The last time Shelley remembered it open was when her mom used to sit on the two cement steps—what they called a porch—years ago. The color in those days, in her memory anyway, was different, less bright. The sky was a paler blue, the bricks of the house liver-toned and the cement just gray. Her mother must not have been thirty yet, but she already had four kids. She was tall and slim, even in loose print dresses. She wore rolled-down white socks and tie-up shoes and her hair was already wife-short. She sat on the little cement square outside the front door trying to teach Boo Boo how to read, her finger tracing words in a book. It had taken days and days, maybe years—Boo Boo had always been slow—and now he was back, a veteran of the Vietnam War, living in Milwaukee. Shelley hardly ever saw him. She couldn't remember if he ever did learn to read right. After having had him around with his big face and slow-apprehending eyes all those years, they should have been friends. The two with something off. But he was the brother who had picked on her. The good-looking ones were always remote and kind.

Everything inside was the same. Her mom cleaning up the kitchen counters, her dad's legs stretched out long and straight like Abe Lincoln's in a chair in front of the tube. There was a playpen set up in there still: her youngest brother's baby.

"Dean and Cath went to the movies," her mother said.

Her father stood up when she came in, patted her shoulder, but then he was back to his show. Her mom was the one who would talk to her. They stood at the end of the house, in the little hall where the linen closet was, between the two bedrooms.

She told her mother she wanted to bring Bill out with her for Christmas. "He doesn't got nobody. Where else can he go?"

"Oh, of all things," her mother said. "Kimmie will be home with the kids. She'd have a cow. People would talk. Like that Bea. She talks." Shelley's mother made a motion with her hand that meant, Blabbermouth.

But it wasn't only gossip that made the women use that gesture for Bea. They all gossiped themselves. So what was it?

Maybe only that she was alone. That she didn't have children. Shelley wasn't sure. But she didn't like her, either. "And he knows her, too," she said. "They eat breakfast together every Thursday."

"I'm telling 'em all at Saint Philip's. I say, 'Naw, she works for him. It's just a job and they're friends, that's all, but it's getting so I don't even know myself. Anyway, he's such a short little poop.'"

Shelley shook her head. "Nothing's doing."

The way her mother looked at her—Shelley had to pinch herself to remember she was telling the truth. All her life, if someone accused her, she felt the ring of a bell deep in her body and she believed it, that what they said was true, it was, and that was why other things were the way they were. She couldn't stop the falling until she was at the bottom of a stone well—cold, slow, almost unable to speak.

Her mother and them, they never guessed about George, but they must have noticed something, and that's where the spot of wrong felt sore.

"You know what they're saying," her mother whispered. "They're saying you're getting to be like a prostitute almost."

"No" was all Shelley could answer.

"Well, I said so, too. And so did Cath. Cath was real mad. She said, 'With a guy that age, he probably can't anymore.' But everyone knows they still want to try."

Shelley went back to the kitchen sink, craned her neck over, and drank from the faucet. The cold water out here tasted good. It was well water, still—what she missed the most living in town.

Then she gave her mom the wrapped boxes with the coffeemaker and all. She told her what was inside, so she wouldn't have to open it right then.

"Jeez, Shelley, it's so much bother," she said.

That was it. No thank-you or anything. And Shelley could tell she wouldn't use it. You knew right away with her mother and a gift. Now, if one of the boys had brought it, that would be a different story.

Even so, Shelley asked Bill Alberts to her family's Christmas, but he declined. He'd go to the Riverclub on Christmas Eve to hear some bass player and then over to Bea Maxwell's house the next morning.

"Though, God knows, the food would be better anywhere else," he said.

XV

When her mother died, for a long time Bea kept busy. She took great care to honor the wishes her mother had expressed regarding the funeral. After all, they'd had a long time to plan. Her mother died June 14, 1984.

She had left detailed preferences, much as, years earlier, she'd organized her parties. She wanted roses, definitely, clustered together in round glass vases, and if there was anything else at all, it should be branches. No ferny things. Or baby's breath, God forbid.

Standing in the back of the florist's, Bea thought of June's store in Arizona. June would get it right away, what her mother wanted. June had always admired Hazel's taste, which even Bea had to admit was somewhat standard. Three or four of the more subtle women Hazel's age wore the same cardigans, chose the same muted shades for their living room drapes. But June's taste—Bea had never seen anything else quite like it. It was almost what you'd have to call a talent. As original as June was, though, she didn't have the confidence Hazel and her friends took for granted. That was a difference, Bea had thought to herself many times since June left. A talent was really something you were born with. Taste had more to do with money, growing up around one kind of furniture you were taught was better than the other kinds.

Her mother had asked for specific music, Schubert songs and an aria from *Lakmé*. Bea told Bill Alberts—her music adviser for many years—and he'd found the musicians. And Lil would play a piano piece by John Robert Poe.

Father Matthew would deliver the eulogy. By the end of her life, Bea's mother would sigh and say, "Too bad he's a priest. Maybe he should just leave, like so many of them do now. Wouldn't *that* be something? Course, then what would he do? He's not really trained in anything. When you think about it, it's not a great background."

Bea shrugged. "How about real estate?"

That was how they laughed together. Small soft jokes that no one else would find funny.

"And look at how well you've done," her mother said. "Really. *Really*."

Maybe, maybe, her mother would've even come around to Bill Alberts.

Talking to Father Matthew about the service, she found herself, for the first time, sitting across a desk from him in his office.

It was a strange room, absolutely silent, lit with the stained-glass windows in muted 1950s colors, muddy pink, brown, and pale green. "My mother and dad," she heard herself saying. "I don't know if they, if they really . . . "

They both sat quiet for a while, absorbed by the peace of the room.

"Raising two children together, living in a house every day, that is a sexual act," Father Matthew finally said.

"She said she missed his warm back at night."

Father Matthew nodded as if this had been expected. But he had known them together, had heard Hazel's exasperation talking about her husband. Surely she had been a dutiful wife. But Bea found herself wondering if there was anything *personal* in it. Sometimes, Bea felt a spike of something—even rage?—but then it subsided as if embarrassed, always unexplained. It would have been important for Hazel to be a good wife. To anyone.

"Maybe she did love him, then," Bea said, a small sob escaping the corner of her mouth, continuing a conversation with herself that Father Matthew was, nonetheless, in his silence, steering. "It was just hard for her to feel that most of the time."

"But she could feel her attachment to you," Father Matthew said. "When she first came to me here, in this room, it was because you'd moved home and she was worried about you. She thought you wouldn't find enough here, after Chicago."

Her mother had selected her own outfit, her own jewels. She was going to be buried in one of Bea's dark brown shawls.

The jewelry became a problem, though. Bea's sister didn't want to bury her in it. "That watch is full of diamonds," Elaine said, here at last, in for the action. Well—the action, so to speak, Bea thought. Her sister hadn't made it in time to see their mother alive.

"Those are *real* pearls," Elaine murmured.

Bea's sister didn't seem to expect or want or try for any experience here. No walk, no conversation that could make a memory. No, her real life was in Minnesota and she was only here to uncover things to take back there. It was as if here she couldn't *feel*. And Bea was a part of what dulled her so.

Her sister was a person who was sure of things. Sure of her life and its importance.

Children, a household, no one would deny that Elaine was living a productive life. But weren't there other things that could matter?

They were in the dim morgue, their mother literally between them, frowning. That frown became an issue later on, too.

"She wants to wear the things our father bought for her," Bea said.

"It's up to you," the undertaker added. "But if it was my mother, I'd think she'd want one of you to get it. Or one of your kids."

Of course Gregg Garsh knew Bea had no children. Everyone was always, in the end, on the side of people with kids. Why was love for children more esteemed than love for parents? Even a man who'd seen you in church every Sunday for the past twenty-five years. And Bea and her mother had always been conscientiously kind to Marge Garsh since the divorce.

After all those evenings, nights when she and her mother sat on their porch looking over the darkening backyard, drinking their tea, now Bea was outnumbered.

Bea tried one more time. "She did select. She gave each of us gifts. But she didn't give us these."

"How old was your ma?" the undertaker asked.

"She was eighty-one, Gregg. I think you know that."

In that way, they won. And because Bea would have none of the dividing or fighting, she let her sister take it all.

She remembered her mother with a three-inch pencil, making notes on a lined card. Bea had tried to see every one of those wishes materialized.

But now she had failed. Her mother's hands were buried bare.

XVI

*B*ea and Bill Alberts met for breakfast every Thursday. At Bosses, they had their own booth. Bill walked, along the river, and was always there, a little before seven, dressed and dapper, sleeves already rolled up, dipping his dry toast in black coffee and reading the newspapers, when Bea arrived. He'd put money on the tabletop jukebox and set it for Nat King Cole's "Route 66."

They talked, ate, and then got to-gos and drove out in Bea's car to see the new listings.

When Jim Dehn handed them their cups from behind the counter, a revolving display of pipes and pipe cleaners, he passed Bea a dime, with a wink.

All week long, she looked forward to Thursday.

Her mother had died and there was an immense stillness in her nights. The eternal conversation, infinitely detailed, had finally ended, leaving Bea in a large house, which seemed itself duller, lackluster.

But every Thursday, she and Bill talked. Often they discussed starting a book club, but they never went about making the necessary plans. Bea didn't take on the task because she felt reluctant to invite others. What if she and Bill didn't like them, once they were in?

Bill Alberts and Bea had June in common. He'd pursued her once, if not for very long; he always was a realist. But he still got a kick out of her adventures and asked after her. When Bea received a letter, she brought it and read the more audacious parts out loud. ("Guess who's blond!" the last one said. "And I *am* having more fun.") They both laughed about her in the same way, glad she was somewhere in Arizona, with her wildflowers and bright colors.

Bea had been surprised and gratified by the finite term of Bill's pursuit of June. It had been pronounced and public, but shorter than his interest in Bea. That alleviated a certain humiliation Bea had felt when it ended. No, even June had not been the grand passion in Bill Alberts's life. That was some consolation, Bea supposed, since she hadn't been, either. It made her wonder if there even was such a thing.

He had one passion and that was jazz.

Green Bay had become a regular stop on musicians' tours, as he'd hoped it would when he'd bought the River-club, though jazz itself, he told her, was becoming rare. Its audience, and not only here, had dwindled. People wanted to hear other things. The younger people wanted rock 'n' roll. Even Tony Bennett was scraping bottom. Most of the crooners were playing wherever they could get a job. Bill himself had played drums for more than forty years. Once, when Benny Goodman's band toured Green Bay, he had filled in for a sick drummer. "Glared at me all night," he told Bea. "Didn't like my playing."

But he had chosen to stay here in Green Bay. "Why did you?" Bea asked one Thursday morning.

"I used to tell my friends I was the only one whose mother worked when he was growing up and the only one who had her living with him now." He waved his hands the same as he had eighteen years ago when he'd hired her. "My sisters left. I was the one to look after them. See my parents into their last beds," he said. "Tuck them in."

Was her reason also his reason? Now, Bea thought, she'd finally gotten the answer to something she'd always wondered. And here the flirt, the womanizer, the putative philanderer had made his life at home in order to take care of his parents.

Bea had seen him drum.

He was one of those musicians who look worst, their most contorted, playing. And yet he played, wanted to play, more than anything. There was something beautiful in it.

After his divorce, he'd never chased Bea again. She was either not pretty enough or not poor enough; she'd never known exactly which. Her mother, of course, had believed it was the latter.

Or maybe it was because he'd already asked, long ago.

Perhaps he'd merely accepted her refusal.

And now Shelley. Shelley who was tootling around town in her new red Jeep, slapping down the platinum credit card he'd given her.

For years, Bea hadn't trusted him because he was a flirt.

And he still was, even with a hip that hadn't healed in the four years since he'd broken it, a prescription that gave him thicker and thicker lenses, and a revoked license that declared him legally blind. She'd wondered if he said the things that he'd said to her to everybody. By now she knew he did, but somehow that didn't seem to make them any less good.

One night at the Riverclub, for a Chamber of Commerce dinner, she recognized his familiar still-headed quality of attention as he listened to the waitress who brought them their drinks. The waitress had a son at home who'd been diagnosed with a condition. Bill wrote the name of a doctor on a napkin and told her he'd call the man tomorrow; the doctor had been one of his mother's students.

He was a flirt, no doubt. But, she found herself wondering, was that so bad? Surely there were worse things. Bea's mother had always said he asked Bea because he knew she had the good sense to say no. What might have warranted a yes?

Was it just another way he flung beauty (white lace handkerchiefs) onto the life they both knew? (Green Bay could certainly use a little.)

To help a waitress command respect from a doctor, to make a real estate agent feel alluring, perhaps this was his compassion.

She ended most Friday evenings with him in the Riverclub, listening to his Cocktail Combo.

One Thursday morning in November, she told him her favorite novel was *Middlemarch*. She'd first read it in college and was reading it again. It was her favorite because the two best people never got together.

"Realistic," he said.

During a phone call from Arizona, June sounded amazed to hear that Bea and Bill Alberts were seeing each other outside the office.

"Just last Friday, he played at the Riverclub," Bea said.

"I hear he's not even very good," June whispered into the phone.

Bea, aghast, felt her breath socked out of her.

What did it matter? To have a lifelong interest like that was admirable, remarkable.

The closest Bea came to that kind of devotion was— what? She wrote to the local government when she thought somebody deserved something. She still rode a bicycle (in brown corduroy knickers), still golfed, still skied. She signed petitions to preserve the city's trees. She knit a blanket and a whole layette for the baby next door. Hundreds of Green Bay houses still displayed her "new home throws." Mostly, she supposed, it had been a life of talking about other people, thinking about love, a kind of love, it turned out, she had never experienced.

At times, she felt that was a failure of hers, some resistance, a hard piece inside her like the stones people got at her age, some mineral blockage. Other times, she thought probably all that would've been fine if she had a slightly more symmetrical face, more space between her top lip and nose.

Most times, she thought it was the world's problem, assuming that everyone had to be two by two, like animals boarding Noah's ark.

Bea supposed she used to be a gossip. June, even with the hardships she'd no doubt borne in the move, her child grown up and gone, had not lost her sly edge. And Bea had. With no attachments to speak of except to a dead mother and her friends.

"You should see me now," June said idly. "I'm unrealistically thin."

Toward the end of the call, when Bea thought it was time to hang up, June kept talking. "Say," she said. "I've got some news. I told you about the person I'm seeing, Hank. Well, he's a very nice man. And we got married. We just did it here at city hall, a Saturday morning, no big fuss or anything. He wanted to. So you're it," she said lightly.

XVII

There had probably been a thousand nights. Alone in the house.

Bea now had her pattern. Home by dark, not before. Those late afternoon hours were deadly.

Not for her the four o'clock walk along the river that Mabel Kaap and her brother had taken every day, looking at the garden flowers. Not that the gardens were so much to see anymore, since the young families had been buying up the old houses and moving in. They were too busy. Both he *and* she worked, and they had kids, too.

Listen, I'm with you, Bea felt like saying. Bea wasn't doing much gardening, either. She felt obliged to keep up her mother's roses, but already the hedges were looking ragged. Rosemary grew like a weed. Maybe it was a weed; Bea didn't know. Her mother had always invited the gardener in for a cold pop. Then she worked alongside him, in her patched pants and English gardening gloves. "If you don't talk to people, you don't get their best work out of them," she always said.

Men pay, Bea thought again; women give gifts. But gift giving was endlessly more complicated.

She had observed her neighbors and clients. Most women still rushed about, yearning for permanence, with unstructured, flighty, busy days. The difference now was that it seemed children—their children's lives—they were trying to perfect, not their homes, or not so much anymore.

Of course, any of these things could be done professionally. You could be a decorator or even an architect if you really wanted to be in the business of making home beauty. You could be a teacher if you wanted to help children, or a camp director, or a librarian. From Bea's experience, professionalism added a note of sanity to most pursuits.

But any of the ladies Bea's mother knew would have been insulted if you'd paid them for what they were doing. She'd made the mistake of trying in her early days, once or twice, as her mother became weak and couldn't keep up the little touches in her house and garden the way she'd liked to. And Bea just didn't have the knack for it. So at first, she attempted the Chicago solution: offer to hire some talented person. Well, that was a mistake. Here, they took it as an insult. Their eye, their taste, their exquisite placements for sale! No, they did it for love, and they most certainly did not love Bea. Once, June had been told, "She asked me to trim her tree. Can you *imagine*?"

The house on Mason had changed since Bea's mother died. Bea had kept Hazel's housekeeper, Beth Penk, but she came only once a week now and Bea answered her own door.

When Bea was young, there had been an old woman, Mrs. Hennigan, who lived two down in the shingled house. She invited everyone in at Halloween for apples and popcorn. Apples and popcorn! Who wanted that?

But the parents made their children stay a respectable

fifteen minutes before running off, disguised, into the wild night. "She's lonely," they explained. "She's all by herself. She doesn't know what kids like."

The neighborhood had changed, turned on its axis, become young again. Strollers and bikes littered the front lawns. A couple from California had moved in next door. The woman was the new local TV anchor. They'd explained to Bea—she'd sold them the Patricks' house—that they didn't intend to stay more than five years. She—the wife—needed experience in what they called "a secondary market." She got up at four every morning and ran out to her car dressed up above the waist, wearing sweats and sneakers below.

Bea liked that. She had read, in *New York* magazine, all about the young women wearing suits, black stockings, and running shoes in the subway on their way to work. Some people had written in against it; others thought it was fine, the only sensible thing.

Her neighbors had two children and he did something at home all day on a computer.

To them, Bea realized, she was the old woman. So she tried not to be like Mrs. Hennigan. She never offered the children anything even vaguely healthy, never inquired about their piano lessons and did they practice?

No, the deadly afternoon hours belonged to children sluffing home from school and gardeners turning on automatic sprinklers. They stretched on, the sunset behind the smokestacks morosely slow, the faint tinkle of the ice-cream truck grinding on your chest.

Bea thought it was just her. Because she was alone and didn't have family. But the dad from next door told her he hated those hours, too, those long hours hanging like wet sheets. "All the moms do," he said. "And I count myself one of them."

Apparently, this had come up in the sandbox. Every day, he packed up the kids and drove to the mall, just to have someplace public to be.

Bea liked to step outside downtown, where people who worked at shops were taking their coffee breaks, talking animatedly about what was going on sale, then walking back to work. No, downtown, it was not the end of the day yet.

She understood why Bill Alberts lingered in his office and then strolled over to Kaap's or Bosses for his dinner.

She'd taken to staying longer, too, hearing the odd note of his jazz come pinging through the open door like a rubber band snapped across a classroom. Some nights, she wandered out with him, both of them carrying papers on clipboards, their work still with them the way their notebooks had been, in college.

As a woman, though, she could not eat out as often as he did. Not if she hoped to keep her shape. She'd spent years building a wardrobe, piece by piece; she wasn't about to start over now, in a size 12 (the size, she'd read, Marilyn Monroe had worn). Most nights she ate a salad at home. She'd learned to make a dressing she liked. Her mother had always just bought dressing at the supermarket. Hazel had been a convenience cook. She'd used lots of cans and mixes—"There's no difference," she used to say derisively about the ridiculous people who insisted on making it all from scratch—and concentrated on spectacular-looking desserts and salads with Jell-O.

Bill Alberts didn't eat out every night, either, not anymore, now that Shelley had become such a cook. Bea had been over there once or twice and seen her barefoot in the kitchen, a bandanna around her head, throwing things into a wok, all without measuring.

Bea usually went to bed with a magazine and a glass of wine. Although it was a large house, Bea lived in it as if it were a one-bedroom.

Most of what she did at home, she did from bed.

Monday was a good night because her *New York* arrived. She would tuck under the covers and try to read slowly, to make it last. It usually took her a full week to work through the Sunday *New York Times*, which they ordered for her at Bosses. She particularly enjoyed the real estate listings in the back of the magazine section. You could hit the million-dollar mark there with one sale, even half of one.

Her long phone calls to June in Arizona took place on top of her comforter, in white pajamas. Bea had taken to calling or, when June phoned, making some excuse to get off and call back in a few minutes—she realized that June was probably worried about the expense. "I need to pee," she liked saying, until June, who, with her portable phone and the time difference, was often at the shop making floral arrangements while they talked, said, "Oh, go ahead and pee. Live a little."

She used to eat in bed, but that had had to stop. Though she'd been careful about crumbs, some ants had come anyway. Her mother had never had ants. In fact, the idea of them had inspired her particular snobbery. "Once you get them, they'll never leave," she'd been fond of warning, believing that their house, built in 1911, had never had a single one.

But Beth Penk, the housekeeper, was older now. Bea still paid her the same salary, but asked that Beth come only Saturdays, when she could be home. The two women sat at the kitchen table and drank a pot of coffee together before the day began.

Bea didn't believe that ants never left. Selling houses, she'd arranged for enough extermination tents, but she was unlikely to go to such measures here. Now. It was an old house. She imagined the ants marching in neat straight lines.

Every so often, Bea wanted to One-Hour Maxwellize her house. She, too, wanted that clean, chemical, *mint* quality. But maybe, she thought, houses were ruined for her. She knew too much about the stagecraft of improvement. Perhaps selling anything eventually spoils it for you.

She'd read once that many prostitutes couldn't enjoy sex. In the same article, it said that most of them refused to kiss their clients, keeping that one small favor for their real boy-friends.

Bea thought to herself that she should have saved back one room to enjoy.

The bedroom. But no, in the houses she listed, she'd done up every part.

One night, she called Father Matthew. Late, for no reason she knew. With no question, no plan, she found herself blabber-ing, trying to improvise. Then, she blurted, "Could you just come over?"

And he said, "Okay, yes. I'll be there."

She got out of bed then, after she hung up, agitated, and started to try to clean her room. Which was where she lived. Which was a mess.

She whirled through piles at a tearing speed. First the bed, then stashing magazines in the closet. Finally it was all done.

And he was still not there.

All of a sudden she remembered his driving. She could see the twin slow headlights moving through the darkened streets; she could draw his car on a map, stopping at every light, waiting at four corner crossings even when there was no other car. For miles.

He's a priest, she told herself, and always will be.

She could imagine the two of them in her neatened bedroom. She could. There would be something mandatory about the act, a certain amount of shame. Heads down, stepping out of trousers. Like children in a locker room, made to change for PE. He would be pale, too, both of them white-legged. They would slow together, not knowing how to move. She thought of Bill Alberts's kick, the way he'd grab her arms and twirl her around, whistling a show tune. Her mother had always said Father Matthew was handsome, but of course she was thinking of him in black and white, in his priest's clothes.

She sighed, heaving herself to the kitchen to measure the ingredients for hot drinks.

She'd have to think fast, concoct some reason for this ridiculous visit.

At her mother's table, pouring the Ovaltine from the warming pot, she dribbled some on his sweater. She dabbed at it with a paper napkin, which shredded on the black. Where was a clean dish towel? When her mother was alive, these things just *stayed* where they should be. The background of the house receded, perfectly, to let you think about nothing but conversation.

Still swabbing at his shoulder, she said, "All these years, have you ever thought of us as . . . "

"Yes. I have," he said, looking down at his lap.

His neck remained in that sloped angle as they drank from their warm cups. Not ten minutes later, he stood up and left.

The way rain makes a path, branching on a windowpane, something started inside Bea, that small a trickle.

The next month, Shelley called up on the telephone. She needed help with *him*. She was driving to Florida; she'd be gone for four days or maybe five. Going to a funeral.

XVIII

Nance was the one who phoned to tell Shelley that George was gone. She called at Shelley's parents' house.

So Shelley heard it from her mother, who told her in a measured-out, cautious voice, afraid to learn any more.

"She just thought you should know," she said. "I told her you can't make it to the funeral, working and all."

"When is the funeral?" Shelley asked.

"Well, it's down there, day after tomorrow. But I told her you've got a job. She doesn't expect you to go all the way to Florida. He never did pay you for all your hours."

Shelley supposed Nance understood some of what had happened.

"I'll go," she said. "I can make it if I drive all night."

The funeral took place in a small cemetery adjoining a golf course. He had already been cremated before Shelley arrived.

"I just don miss him," Nance said out in the bright air, sounding as if that were a thing to wonder about. She kept shaking her head, amazed.

He had been hard with her; Shelley didn't doubt it.

At the end, Nance had had to do everything for him, even when he went to the bathroom, Petey told her.

Petey—now a middle-aged man with a beard, wearing a Hawaiian shirt—said that dressing George took an hour and then, when it was done, he'd kick his legs and pummel his arms, shouting, "No, no, not this. Take it off." Nothing was ever right.

Shelley nodded. "I used to say to him, 'Who made you God?' "

"Yah," Petey said. "You knew him all right. Built that pool." He shook his head. "She went through a lot with him."

"But she never stood up to him, though," Shelley said. "There's probably ten tape measures with my skin on 'em around your old place, but see, I'd throw it back at him. There's the difference."

"He tore the phone out," Petey said.

"I s'pose" was all she finally answered. She shook her head. "To build up a place like that."

She remembered his telling her she could go there any-time. He couldn't imagine dying. Not then. And that wasn't so long ago. Fifteen, sixteen years.

"Well, you did it with him," Petey said. "I wasn't gonna."

Now Nance was going around with an old guy who was from Green Bay, too. They had worked together at Kendalls—in the notions department—before she was mar-ried, forty years ago. And they both loved Florida.

"So you don't miss Green Bay at all?" Shelley said.

"With this weather," Nance said, "I could never go back. You know, I got pains in my hands. The tops. Like an oval disk. Right here."

Shelley had heard about this. When you were a nurse,

people told you their ailments. She picked up Nance's hands. They were small and plump, with fancy pink nails and age spots. She began to rub them. "But the sun makes it better?"

"Yah, the heat helps. Up there, I was getting so I just stood by the grate. Here it melts away."

"Then you should stay," Shelley said.

XIX

*B*ea cleaned the house, just in case. Her mother's home had been a landmark on the garden tour when Hazel was alive. But that was coming undone. . . .

When she told Bill Alberts she'd be staying with him or that he could move in with her, he moaned. "I'll let you escort me home from the club," he said.

The first night, he let her drive him and walk him to his door. That was it. The second night, no more. The third night, which for all she knew would be the last, Bea worked herself up to say something.

Her key was still in the ignition, the two of them just sitting there.

"When we were younger . . . ," she began.

"When *you* were young," he corrected. "*I* was never young."

"Our friendship, I thought our friendship could've gone a different way." She was looking straight ahead, out the windshield at his house. "But now—"

"It's too late for me," he said, a hand on her shoulder.

For a minute they sat there, cold in the car.

"Well, okay," she finally said, "let's go, then." She got out her door and closed it and let him get out on his own.

She blamed him. He'd once liked her, maybe even loved her, but not enough, not enough to wait. What? Seventeen years. "So whatever you felt then," she said, turning half back at him, "not anymore. Kaput."

"I've always believed in you. I still do that."

Then he fell, climbing the shallow steps made of river stones.

"Oh," she said, getting down to help him. She'd let this happen, out of spite, and he was old, older than her father was when he died. A sharp mineral smell slammed up at her from the ground.

Her hands were under his arms, trying to haul him up, and he wasn't budging. Then, all of a sudden, he laughed.

"What are we doing?" he said.

Oh no, she thought. She didn't want it to stop. So she didn't say anything. Most often in her life, she'd harmed things with too much talking. *Cluck, cluck, cluck, cluck*—she knew what they said about her. She imagined nothing would change if she just kept her clap shut.

He was the same man as always, still himself, his eyes intent. But his face seemed softer somehow, around the mouth. His hands were large and flat, like a mime's implying walls as he grazed the outside points of her.

"At our age," he finally said, a continuation but also an answer to his own question.

XX

*B*ill had been asked to look into the Belgian monastery property. "They want to sell off their orchards," he said, handing Bea the papers the next morning. "They have a second mortgage. It's your religion. Better you than me."

"I'm not Catholic," Bea snapped. Given how he was looking at her, Bea understood she'd not only been a gossip but also the subject of it. People probably believed she'd been the priest's mistress. But did *he* think so?

"Well, Christian, I meant," he said, hands up flat. "Falling on hard times and selling off their orchards. Very Chekhov."

The monastery's prime hillside estate ran all the way down to the river, bordered on one side by Heritage Hill, the town's historical society, and on the other by the old orphanage. Next to that was the penitentiary with its four walls and corner watch towers, where, not so long ago, at night, you could see the silhouettes of guards holding rifles. First they called it a penitentiary, then the reformatory. Now it was supposed to be the Wisconsin Correctional Facility.

Bea drove over to see the abbot. It was no surprise that the order was broke. Novitiates, she knew from Father Matthew, were scarce. From a community of over a hundred, in the last decade the population of the Norbertine Abbey had dwindled to fewer than forty. And most of them were old. When Bea's mother was growing up, it was not uncommon for one son from large Catholic families to enter the monastery. "But then," she'd said, "I suppose they had enough to spare." Even when Bea was in high school, she knew one girl whose older brother, a handsome boy, was becoming a priest. He'd had a girlfriend, a beautiful girl named Marie, but he told her that after graduation he was going into the abbey. That was when all her trouble started. Later on, he dropped out anyway. But by then she was working at the bank; she'd cut off her shining hair.

Bea had a plan. Heritage Hill—of which she was a long-standing board member and a docent, donning the costume of an 1850s matron, replete with butter churn and apron, every year for the Christmas festival—would buy the orchards and the fields, and the brothers could continue to tend their vines and trees, to make their honey and candles forever, to use the land as if it were theirs. It just wouldn't be, technically, anymore.

She met Father Matthew in the monastery's plain kitchen, probably renovated sometime in the 1950s and never updated. Supermarket bread waited in its bag on the counter, next to generic brands of peanut butter and jelly.

Two guests sat with him at the table. There was a Dutch priest who had just completed an eight-month walking trek through Italy; he spoke no English, Father Matthew explained. And also the girl he'd told her about before—a runaway he was trying to help, named Dawn. He'd found her a second or third foster home, but little as she had, she didn't like the responsibility of family life. The foster families had assigned her chores, expecting her to pitch in and help baby-sit.

Bea noticed the girl's bare foot up on her chair, the dull and scratched skin, her dingy hair.

On the windowsill were two tomatoes and an avocado, not yet ripe, in a long triangle of sun. All these years, she'd never pictured the inside of where he lived.

Father Matthew led Bea to the abbot, who met her in the room where she'd sat planning her mother's eulogy.

The abbot jumped up and shook her hand with such vigor that it seemed to Bea unseemly, a man of God kowtowing to a realtor.

She laid out the plan with all its paperwork. She was proud of her solution, if she did say so herself. It had taken hours of round-robin phone calls to the Heritage Hill board members, who were not all so eager to pay top dollar to the monks. Bea had convinced them with the sobering fact that if they didn't buy, there were no zoning restrictions to prevent the abbey from selling to a developer, who could put up condominiums, which would certainly impinge on their nineteenth-century view.

The abbot, however, didn't seem to glean the miracle of board approval. "But then we wouldn't own the property?" he said for the second time.

"No, you wouldn't own it. You're selling it. That's why they're paying you all this money. But you'd have a perpetual lease, for one dollar a year, so your bees, your apricots, and everything will be hunky-dory."

"But we won't own it," he said again.

You people aren't supposed to believe in owning anyway, she wanted to scream. You sure don't for your nuns! A year or so earlier, there'd been a flurry in the local news when a landlord sold the building that housed seven or eight elderly nuns. The retired women—Bea's neighbor, the TV anchor, had reported—were impoverished and had nowhere to go. Several were writing to relatives in different states, whom they hadn't seen for years. "Retired?" Bea had said to her. "Well, not from nunship," she'd answered, "but teaching. They used to all be teachers."

"It's just hard to sign a paper saying that we won't own our land."

Hard, but he did.

Bea stopped by the kitchen to say good-bye to Father Matthew.

"Do you ever miss, like, going out with somebody?" Dawn was asking.

The girl's blond hair held a tinge of green.

"People ask me if I need physical contact," Father Matthew said. "And I do. I need hugs."

The way the slim girl kept peering, Bea was quite certain his answer had not satisfied her.

"What about more than hugging?" Dawn suggested, blowing on her tea, holding the mug up near her face with two hands. Both feet were on the chair, her knees pulled up to her chest.

"Oh, if I get my hugs, I'm all right," he said.

XXI

$\mathcal{A}$fter the funeral, Shelley ate with them all at Big
Boy and then got back up in the Jeep and drove the
forty-one hours home, stopping for food and coffee at rest
stops.

She pulled into Green Bay at ten o'clock, and the air was
soft, wet, dark. She parked in the lot at the Riverclub and
went right up. At ten o'clock, he was usually still there.

"Oh, hello," he said. "I thought I was out a truck and
a girl."

Shelley still flicked her foot. The habit drove her mother nuts.
At Christmas, she'd said, "People won't hire you if they see
you doing it. They'll think you're crazy." (She used to say,
"Kids won't want to play with you.")

"I already got a job."

"And what do you think is going to happen when he dies?"

For some reason, Shelley found herself repeating this
conversation to Bill Alberts at the Riverclub, right after
she loped in. It kept coming to her as she steered the long
way back.

Bill Alberts was quiet, sipping his drink, which was only water; as long as she'd known him, he hadn't touched the stuff. Then he said, "I'm worried, too."

" 'Bout me?"

"About what you'll do when I die."

"What, you think I'm crazy, too? Anyway, you planning on croaking sometime soon?"

"I'm seventy," was all he said. Then he sighed. "You know, I'd be glad to pay for a psychiatrist. Dr. Klicka, over on Baird, probably the best we have here. Best and only."

"So you do think I'm nuts."

"I went to Dr. Klicka myself for more than a decade. We still play chess. You've seen her. You know her as Katie."

"*You* did? What for?" The idea of a rich person needing a head doctor was altogether new to Shelley. Even her mother would know better, from the magazines.

"I'm afraid you'll be too alone. I've noticed you don't like to go over to your family very often."

"I don't love my parents," she said. "I loved my grandmother."

A few minutes later, Bea Maxwell dashed in, dressed up, holding her keys out. There was something about her that Shelley couldn't put her finger on. But it was him *with* her, too. They were laughing together like her parents had, long ago.

Both standing, they danced a few steps, Bill almost tipping her over, Bea was so much taller.

That night in the kitchen, giving him his medications, Shelley tried to start something. She stood behind him, rubbing his shoulders a way she'd done before, but then her head went straight forward like a turtle's, her face near to his face.

"Nothing doing," he said. "You ought to be ashamed."

But Shelley was not ashamed, not then. Lots of people, she'd noticed, had one problem or another with sex. Or maybe most people had the same problem.

But in that one thing, Shelley was lucky. She didn't wear out on a person like her sister Kim did and get exasperated all the time. And she was not afraid of them leaving, either. She didn't clutch at people or drive them crazy, as she'd seen the less pretty of her brothers' girlfriends try. She knew that George had needed her, and that Bill Alberts did now.

She just wanted to keep what she had.

"Okay, I'm ready," he said.

Bill had told her once that he'd never adjusted to sleeping downstairs. He missed his old bedroom. There were trees that made sounds out that window; the acoustics were better. So every night now, Shelley heaved him over her shoulder and carried him up to his old room. He always gave her a shawl to drape on her shoulder first, so they didn't exactly touch.

Mornings, he could get down himself, clutching the banister.

The next morning was Thursday, his early day. He was out before she was up. But he'd left her a card with Dr. Klicka's phone number on the breakfast table.

"The only doctor I'd go to is one that could fix my foot," she said out loud. "And even God probably can't do that."

XXII

$\mathcal{J}$he first Thursday morning when Bill Alberts didn't show up at Bosses, Bea waited until eight o'clock. They'd never made a plan in case one of them didn't come. They were both always there.

She mostly knew already. She was just letting it find her, maybe trying to outrun it a little. After all, it might be nothing. A person could be ill or oversleep. The man *was* seventy. And it wasn't like that Shelley to heave herself up and deliver a message.

Heads snapped when Bea Maxwell swung into the office at this hour, with a large take-out cup of coffee from the expensive chain that had recently opened on Madison Street. Bea did not keep regular hours—not because she'd entered a partial retirement, although, at her age, that would not have been out of the question. But no, Bea Maxwell was not the retiring type. Tall, vigorous, a regular golfer in the round-robin tournaments at the club, she had taken care of her mother until she died, and she had no children. Never married. She was stylish, in a way that made some people in town more suspicious than impressed, and others merely hopeful for her. "Well, but she keeps herself up," they said.

No. Bea Maxwell had no children and only a formal and frosty connection to her sister's children, who no longer even came for their annual pilgrimage from Minnesota in the station wagon, now that the grandmother was dead and buried (and her will, presumably, long ago executed, already in their stone Minnesota banks). Bea was already at the age when some Green Bay people speculated about her own will. The Minnesota children? Most figured it would all go to June Umberhum's girl, who would be grown already, through college.

Never married. It was fair to say that of Bea now. She was now someone who had never married, not someone who had just not married yet. Once, in her thirties, she and her mother had been terribly offended when a lady at the bromeliad society said it was a shame Bea hadn't married, because she was so good with children. They had always assumed, of course, that she would. She still would.

Then, after not one moment but an unremarked cluster of days and seasons, that was over. And now it was done. She had not.

Bea would continue selling houses, running the board at Heritage Hill, knitting shawls and playing in tournaments at the club for some time. She would listen to classical music on National Public Radio and also, now, to jazz, mostly Ella Fitzgerald and Oscar Peterson. She would hire local boys to mow the lawn at her mother's house, where she had grown up and still lived. She would write her letters, generally of the unanswered kind, to local newspapers and even the mayor's office, to put in her two cents about what she thought was wrong.

Probably, too, she would continue her twice-annual shopping trip to Chicago, as long as she could, although the motive for these expensive clothes had shifted slightly. If she had once cultivated a dramatic style to lure the attentions of eligible Green Bay men, she had by now become accustomed to compliments on her attire, to women looking to see what she was wearing this season. Women her age and older, that was.

She had kept up a subscription to *New York* magazine for as long as she could remember, although she had never actually been to New York. But she sent away for things. Clothes sometimes arrived in long shipping cartons, certain foods; special yarn from Italy came in boxes with yellow stamps. Her last extravagance had been ice cream made with tea leaves and rose petals, delivered to her door packed in dry ice. She'd invited her neighbors—with the children—in for that.

No. Bea Maxwell kept eccentric hours because she could. She'd made the million-dollar mark for the first time in 1971 and twice in the 1980s, when everywhere, even Green Bay, was feeling the boom economy. She was good at her job, and nobody in the office would dare deny it.

Also, and this was unsaid, Bea had grown up here, on Mason Drive, she'd attended De Pere High. Her father was the revered Dr. Maxwell. Everyone had known her parents and the house they lived in.

Now, she breezed into her office—"Morning, Edith. How's the leider coming? And how's Grace?"—a corner with a shivering bright Japanese maple out the long window.

Other agents and secretaries, even the accountant, had certainly noticed that the two best offices were empty most of the time, but this observation provoked little more than sighs.

No one would've thought of saying anything to Bill, or to Bea, for that matter.

This morning, she took a letter from her purse, on frail onionskin paper, with colorful stamps. It was from Peggy, June's daughter, who was traveling in India, taking photographs.

She'd written Bea almost a month ago, to see what had happened to her grandmother's house. She didn't know if she could afford it, she wrote, but she wanted to buy it when it came up for sale. She said in Nepal, she had had a dream that she was living there in that house, as a grown-up, with a daughter of her own.

Her grandmother's house! Surely she would've heard about that by now, even in India. June would know, from Nance, if no one else. But there was, Bea supposed, always the chance that June and her sister-in-law weren't talking. That night when Shelley had clomped into the Riverclub smelling like a truck driver, Bea had asked what June was wearing at the funeral. Shelley had just stared at her awhile, her features sharp—the stare of a bird—and then said June wasn't even there.

Her own brother. The idea caused a shiver to run through Bea—of horror and exhilaration. Even as out of touch as Bea was with her sister, she imagined they'd be standing there at each other's funerals. Bea would be, anyway. She couldn't not. Still, Bea hadn't heard from her sister in over three years, discounting Christmas cards—mere Polaroids of the kids, without even such a thing as a human signature.

It was not even nine o'clock yet, but Bea had done a little research. And she already had an idea. Across the road from June's mother's house was another little house. Shelley owned that now.

Bea stood with an uptake of breath and walked by his office. The door was open, the desk with everything as it had been yesterday. He still had the copper vase he'd paid June to fill with flowers every week until she left town. It stood there in its own place, dry.

"No Bill?" she asked Edith, who was sitting up straight, typing. Behind her, on the blackboard, it said: *There are three sides to every controversy; yours, the other person's, and the right side*.

"I don't know where he is. It's Thursday. He's usually with you."

"Probably a late night at the club," Bea said.

But it wasn't a late night. Bea had been there. He'd gotten up to do a short set himself, his head wagging, the tongue loosening out a little. Then they'd all headed home at ten-thirty, Bea in her own car, him up high in Shelley's Jeep.

Bea pushed through the front door. She'd drive out to Keck Road so she could answer Peggy's letter properly. She'd send it today, then tonight write a longer one to June.

In the early 1980s, when there was so much building going on all around, a subdivision opened the fields past the railroad tracks that crossed Keck Road. First one nursery bought out the other, then a developer targeted both parcels. Bill Alberts had been one of the partners. They had put up earth-toned two stories, each with its own tree and fenced-in yard. Bea had been put in charge of the fixtures and appliances. She'd hired Mr. Campbell's protégé, a local boy named Buddy Janson, who'd been to the Twin Cities and come back. He picked out all the tile and paint colors. They did such a good job on that, Bill put Bea in charge of landscaping too. The city paved the roads. A school bus route was charted. Bill Alberts had made another fortune.

A whole new kind of person lived in those houses now, couples mostly, with young children, who were not from here, but from towns farther out. To them, even there off 141, this was coming to the big city.

And now the old houses on Keck Road were beginning to come down. Well, it was time. Forty, fifty years old, most of them were. As old as she was. After all, Keck, the son of a Milwaukee brewer, had opened the road and named it after himself, in nineteen ought six.

One of Bea's favorite mottoes was *The only thing that works around an old house is the owner.* She'd always lived by these words, renting apartments in new buildings and eventually buying the condo. Now that she'd inherited her parents' brick Georgian, she knew her old saying to be true.

Last year, Wal-Mart bought out what had been June's mother's land, as well as George and Nance's, from the people who'd bought from them.

Nance would have heard by now, even in remotest Florida, and would she ever be mad. Again, Bea congratulated herself on her restraint. Nance would not be beyond suing the broker. Nowadays, Bea had read, brokers were taking out insurance. Edith had a small placard on her reception desk. *If we'd only held on to it—Famous Last Words.*

It would be a good thing, anyway, to take a look. Since the Wal-Mart deal, she'd received calls from owners on the other side of the road. They all wanted to sell. Of course, who would want to live across from a huge parking lot where there used to be a hundred-year-old oak? But at the same time, they didn't want to sell their houses for what they were worth, either.

They wanted to get the big mall money without hanging on and waiting. It was just like the owners who cashed out, selling their houses when the market was high and then complaining because they had nowhere to live.

Bea didn't know if the houses were even still there. Maybe they'd already broken ground. She took along a camera to snap some pictures for Peggy.

She had a golf game at one o'clock. She could make it back home in time to shower and change.

Highway 141 was built up now, and very different from the development on the West Side. Every kind of fast food castle was here, standing on small adjacent lots. Arby's and Taco Bell surrounded the old Kroll's. Friendly's, Big Boy, IHOP.

June used to like the strawberry pie at Big Boy, one of the first chains, an old one. That was June. Bea avoided all the drek, but June, like Bea's own mother, had been able to enter the world as if it were a huge bazaar and just pick and choose.

Bea was turning now onto Keck Road. But for the small sign, she wouldn't have recognized the corner. The farmhouse on one side had changed into some kind of bank. The tavern, apparently, was long gone.

It was May, the branches rich with bright green buds, so beautiful it made her ache, for no reason that she knew, except not being young.

She was driving up the still-bumpy road, passing the bad house, now plain gray, probably six owners later, but the place had kept its junk, the hood of an old Chevrolet and other rusted car parts littering the front yard.

And then there it was, like a prison yard. An endless lot marked off by a chain-link fence. The houses were mostly down. A little crowd of children had gathered to look, fingers in the tin diamonds of the fence. There was a fire. A fire truck inside the enclosure was stalled at a diagonal. Bea parked across the road. She supposed you could park here. There were still no sidewalks and nothing saying you shouldn't.

George's house was completely down, only the outline of its foundation still visible, but his jerry-built cabana was half standing. There was water in the pool, a murky shade of brown-green. June's mother's house was gone and the huge tree was burning. Bea was transfixed. She'd never seen a tree on fire. The branches were sprouting large flames and it seemed the trunk was on fire, near the top. Dense horizontal branches were growing black and she could see silver cracks forming as if in slow motion. One limb fell with a huge noise; then a black cloud of cinders bounced off the ground. Four firemen stood behind a hose, aiming at the flames. They looked like Keystone Kops, slow, not quite real. Their voices held none of the bright clarity of fear.

Someone was touching her on the left side, and Bea realized it was Shelley.

"What happened?" Bea asked.

"First, they were going to move the houses," Shelley said. "But then they had to have the land cleared by the end of the month. So they're just lettin the fire department use it for practice. They set the tree on fire. They'll put it out and then do it over again. My mom went before and took out everything valuable. Doorknobs. Appliances. Whatnot."

She stood with her hands in her pockets. There seemed no use for her strength. "That beautiful pool," she said. "I'm glad he isn't here to see it."

The letter from Peggy was folded in Bea's purse. *I should have written earlier but I was just—what?—disorganized, I suppose.*

Peggy would be sorry about the house. That was mostly sentiment. But what was worse was the tree. Bea remembered it bare and enormous, laden with snow, when she'd first come down this road. It would have been unthinkable to her then that the tree wouldn't be here forever. Soon people would come who'd never even known it had been here.

Once, there must have been trees that old all around, where her own house now stood, on the cobbled streets of pretty brick shops, florists, and quaint cafés.

"I have a letter from Peggy Umberhum, June's daughter. She wanted to buy her grandmother's house."

"Sheesh. Too late now, huh?"

"I was wondering if you'd want to sell your house here." Bea nodded toward the small blue house across the road. "They're similar properties. Same era, same size."

"You mean my gramma's house? Heck, I can't sell that. My brother and them are there. I told them they want it, they can have it." She stepped back. Shelley had the appearance of someone who had always been very tall and narrow and who simply wasn't narrow anymore, even in the well-cut slacks Bill Alberts had no doubt selected.

"Did you know I was here?" Bea asked.

"Followed you out," Shelley said. "So—Peggy Umberhum, huh? Jeez Louise."

"You probably knew each other from when you were little."

"Wese played together. Then for a long time, I didn't see

her." She stood surveying the distant fields, where the roofs of the Vandermill Houses could be seen. "We was kids once."

After a while, she said, "So, you selling many houses out here?"

"Some. Here, it's mostly development. And I get the odd duplex here and condominium there."

"You got land for sale, too?"

"Oh, sure. Some people would rather build."

"I wanna buy some land up north. Anywheres with well water. I don't like the taste of Green Bay water. And it's getting too crowded for me around here."

"Well, that's not going to help," Bea said, nodding to the site in front of them. She felt the heat wafting over her arms. Before too long, there'd be a girl younger than Shelley who would step up in a uniform and say, "Can I help you?"

"My sister Kim says if I think Green Bay's crowded, I should see Tokyo."

"Or New York."

"I never been there."

"No, I haven't, either," Bea said.

They started walking. "See if my folks are there. I can use their stuff to make us coffee." Her parents weren't home, but their side door was open. The cement porch was surrounded by thistles, Queen Anne's lace, and long grass. Their steps set insects jumping.

Shelley took out a brand-new coffeepot from a box, washed it out under the tap, and began to brew coffee.

When it was finished, they took their mugs out into the backyard. The view there was probably the same as it had always been. They could see the chimneys of the slaughterhouse, and the air was pungent, not necessarily bad, a hospital smell, sugary and somehow warm.

Shelley's coffee was good, as good as the new expensive place on Madison where everyone paid $2.50 for a cappuccino.

There was a careful, tended garden, marked off with pine stakes and white string, the vegetables in rows: carrots, parsley, peas, different lettuces.

"Did your mother always keep a garden?"

"Oh, sure," Shelley said. "He liked the taste of her stuff, too. I started coming to get fresh peas. I even had her planting the herbs he liked."

"I know you're a good cook," Bea said. "Not just from what Bill says, but once he brought a scrumptious rhubarb pie you made into the office."

"Oh, that," she said, looking down. "I was just trying to make it taste the way we ate rhubarb out here."

Why did she look embarrassed?

"How was that?"

"Oh, just we cut it with a knife and our ma would give us a little pile of sugar on a plate. We'd dab it in and eat the stalk. The way kids do. Sugar'd get all pink. Yah, they didn't cook anything fancy. We'd just stand there and eat peas off the vine."

On a clothesline tied between two pines hung clean T-shirts, white and navy blue, white socks, underwear, flannel button-downs, and big, long jeans.

"I bet your parents married for love," Bea said. That was what she'd thought looking at the neat display of laundry, and it just came out.

"Round here, back then, there wasn't much else to get married for. None of thems had any money."

There was a new redwood structure in the backyard, an octagonal enclosed porch, walled with window screens.

"They can sit at night outside without the bugs. Hear the birds," Shelley said, opening the door.

And inside this rough octagon, the sound did seem different. The noise from across the road hushed. Thinner sounds magnified. Birds became individual, single voices.

They sat on the wooden furniture Shelley's father had built.

"So you want to leave Green Bay," Bea said.

"Yah. I like it like it was around here when we was growing up."

"I remember it, too," Bea said. "I used to come out and pick up June. When I first saw June's house, I was surprised. She told me she came from a poor family. I'd only known her at college. And then it was so beautiful out here."

"If they was poor," Shelley said, "I don't know what that makes what we were."

Bea looked at Shelley, remembered the baby she'd once seen, and considered her life for possibly the first time.

"You may get married and have kids," Bea said softly. "And you'll want to raise them somewhere with land like this."

Shelley closed her mouth in a small, mocking smile. "Not me, not anymore."

"Why not?" Bea asked.

But she didn't answer.

What was she? Twenty-five? Maybe thirty? "It's not too late for you." Bea actually touched the girl's hand. It was long and hard as a man's.

Shelley looked at her with no expression; then a large smile cracked open. "I got a place to sell."

"Another place? Oh, well."

"You know the Kaap house?"

"The Kaap house. Oh." Bea couldn't help but whisper, "He died, then."

"Oh boy, I thought you knew. They called me from the police. Found him a block from Bosses, sitting on a wall by the sidewalk. Just somebody's yard. They said he must've felt a pain and stopped to rest. The lady who lives there found him when she went out to get her paper. All dressed up like he was going somewhere important, she said. Just his head down and his clothes all soaked from sweat. Holy smokes." She frowned. "He knew I'd sell it. When he told me he was giving it, I said, 'Well, don't expect me to live there and clean that whole thing. All them floors.'"

He left her the house! The Kaap house! Bea heard the old familiar ring in the air—her gossip's instinct—but there was no one left to tell, leaving this silver fact limp, useless.

June was gone and her mother was gone, too, all her listeners. The women she'd been able to make laugh.

"But there was nothing going on between us. He was just doin it to be nice."

Bea looked up at the girl, who was biting her bottom lip.

If June were still around to call, if her mother were here, Bea wouldn't have looked at the girl again and seen—what she saw now—a crooked face telling the truth. Of course, Bea reminded herself, she was the only one who'd believe it.

"You can take what you want of those books or the records. CDs. I never could understand that music. He always said you got his jokes. I'm just going to box that all up for the church. There's an envelope with your name on it, too, on his desk. Some kind of ticket with something hard in it. His watch, maybe."

"Well, you helped him," Bea said. "Made his last years kinder."

Bea supposed that was what she had done for her mother. And here she was with that house.

And Shelley was planning to sell. With the money, she wanted to buy up where the water tasted better.

She pointed out the bushes planted along the screens. They were all hollies that fed the birds.

Shelley offered to take her for a drive in the red Jeep. They could head north, look at some land. Bea got in carefully, a hand on the roof as she clambered up the high running board.

Before, she may have wondered—certainly her mother would have—how it looked to be Shelley's passenger in this vehicle everyone knew who'd paid for.

But today she opened the window. Inside, they were very high up, with wide views. Her hair, which she'd set all her life to straighten, was probably blowing right now into curls.

A NOTE ON THE TYPE

This book was set in Caledonia, a typeface designed by W. A. Dwiggins (1880–1956). It belongs to the family of printing types called "modern face" by printers—a term used to mark the change in style of the type letters that occurred around 1800. Caledonia borders on the general design of Scotch Roman but is more freely drawn than that letter.

Composed by Stratford Publishing Services,
Brattleboro, Vermont

Printed and bound by R. R. Donnelley & Sons
Harrisonburg, Virginia

Designed by Dorothy S. Baker